THE BISHOP'S BEARD

ARTHIA NIXON

I0621591

"OMG! SO MUCH triggers and truth TO UNPACK!"

"I was cussing everybody but the kids from chapter one!"

"Girl, 'Elevators' was hot, this is hell in the pulpit!"

"I thought I knew the secret but then came the bombshell, now I can't even breathe!"

"That church hurt, tho!"

"Thia, this needs to be a movie!"

THE BISHOP'S BEARD

ARTHIA NIXON

AMBASSADOR
agency

Printed in the United States of America
Cover design: Franny Henderson
Editorial assistant: Linda A. Duncombe
www.ArthiaNixon.com

This is a work of fiction. Names, characters, businesses, events and incidents are the products of the author's imagination. Any resemblance to actual persons, living or dead, or actual events is purely coincidental.

ISBN 978-1-7349861-6-7
Royal Ambassador, LLC

To 'Olo'. Thank you for choosing me and for the memories and deep secrets. May we continue in faith, walking in purpose and truth, being richly blessed, overcoming and "in it together - always".
Thank you also Linda A. Duncombe for your encouragement.
Cheers to trapsiness lol
Also to you Lexi and you know why xoxo

CHAPTER 1

"Fuck this church," Judah muttered as he made his way to the pulpit in the midst of the commotion.

The video was already on the main monitors and obviously shared on the phones.

"Whoever is in the media room, shut this shit down now!" he shouted into the microphone. "And cut the livestream. Everyone calm down."

"Well I came to worship not see you and your wife's sex tape!" a deaconess stood.

"Girl, that was her but it wasn't him," another woman said.

The congregation of Greater Gates was out of control and Judah Waters had no way of reeling it back in. His entire life had changed in the past year and it all culminated to this point. He should have focused on music in California instead of trying to be a superhero in Georgia at his parents' church. Now it was all in the open - the scandal, the lies, the deceit. And he was the only one who could fix it. But with a thousand people staring at him waiting for a response, he had to say something and quickly.

"Sin in the camp!" someone shouted from the congregation. "Sin is in the camp!"

"Sin in the camp and you're in the camp so that means you ain't nothing but another sinner in the camp!" someone else shouted back.

"Well I'm leaving this hell hole!" another person called. "I am not going to be covered by a church that has all this foolishness at the head. Y'all all going to hell. My soul ain't joining a one of you! That's what happens when you give the church to a musician."

Judah's palms were sweaty as he held onto the pulpit amid the shouting in Greater Gates Church. He felt his chest tightening and his collar choking him. He looked at the photos of the church's bishops on the wall and stared for a moment at the photo of his brother, Josiah. So much had changed within a year. So much. He'd been given an assignment and failed it. Now his family and church was paying the price.

He felt a gentle hand cover his, and suddenly felt the courage to open his eyes again.

"Now, everybody is going to calm down and we are going to hear the truth," Judah found his voice.

"Oh, I don't have to stay here for this," someone else got up.

"Sit down and hush up!" Judah commanded. "Now all y'all just calm down. I didn't want to have to go here but enough is enough. Everyone in here has sin. And I am not going to let you all attack each other."

"We ain't attacking each other," a voice shouted at him. "We just want *that* woman gone! Cast her out!"

Judah looked at his wife Dericka as she gave his hand a squeeze.

"We stick together…" she said. "Whatever, you decide. I trust you to make the right decision even if that means parting."

Unbeknownst to each other, their minds flashed back to about a year ago when this life was one they never thought they'd be living. They both recalled his last night of normalcy. It was thousands of miles away in a packed stadium when he was known as Judah 3:16 and completely in his element on a stage singing.

"Everybody just lift your hands in worship…" Judah would close his eyes and raise his hand while the musicians took his cues. "You deserve it all Lord. Get personal and let's give him all the glory and honor and praise. Don't worry about your neighbor right now. This is your personal moment."

Judah had a way of speaking and singing that made people stop and listen. As the cymbals, drums, guitar, and keyboard players joined in, the energy in the stadium shifted into a mood from praise to worship. The backup singers were so connected to Judah's leads and ad-libs one would think it was intentional. Especially Ruby. She was the one Judah relied on to keep the vocalists on point on and off the stage. He personally picked every member of his team and thought he had created something magical. This was Judah 3:16, winning awards in secular and gospel industries, and winning souls while connecting sounds, traditional and contemporary.

Then there was Pastor Judah when it was formal even though he repeatedly told people to simply refer to him as Judah. His background in the Baptist community had folks calling him pastor before he was ordained. He stood tall, with mocha brown skin, a handsome, chiseled face with a trimmed beard, fit body, and keen fashion sense. In spite of the faith aspect, he still made women forget themselves and they were drawn to him in droves.

The live concerts were always his best moments where he flawlessly delivered. He had that flow one couldn't teach in music school, a skill that was acquired only with a solid faith-based upbringing and constant companionship with elders in the music ministry. It was the mark of a leader, a psalmist and a music minister who could create an atmosphere that couldn't be explained as anything other than otherworldly. Tears flowed, decrees and declarations made and people were so caught up in the moment, confessing sins, shouting praises and falling out, they didn't realize an hour could go by.

Judah cleared his throat after hitting a high note, prompting a voice in his earpiece to give directions.

"Judah, transition off stage, take a breather and drink something and let Shay sing a solo and from here on out, Ruby has the high notes," Derika ordered as she made her way to where he would come off stage. "Cue her in now Judah."

Judah continued to sing.

"Ruby, if you can hear me raise your hand, please," Derika spoke again.

Ruby raised her hand as if she was in the middle of a hallelujah shout.

"Judah don't play with me or else I will mute you," Derika warned.

Ruby and the band took it down a notch and Judah smiled. His name was on the marquee but they knew Derika called a lot of the shots.

"Shay… come here," Judah turned to a young woman from his backup singers.

Still in her teens and a bit nervous when called out, Shay never questioned Judah and made her way to him. She was short in height with lots of curly hair and bright eyes eager to take in new experiences.

"How you doing Shay?" he asked, putting an arm around her as if he were a father displaying a child who made him proud.

"I'm good," she said quietly.

"You got to talk into the mic so they can hear, baby girl," he told her, making the audience laugh.

"You ain't gotta do me like that," she laughed along.

"Y'all don't mind her pretending she can't speak, this baby girl can sang!" Judah said as Shay blushed hearing the applause. "Ladies and gentlemen, this is my goddaughter Shay Sanchez and it's her very first tour, amen. Could sing before she could talk, this one here. I finally let her sing with the choir at church when she was about seven, and my wife, that beautiful lady with the earpiece walking around making sure we all stay in line, my wife agreed that it is time to share our Shay with the world. She's been with us for the summer, and she was playing around in my studio at home and got caught singing. I mean sanging. So I figured well you're in my house eating up my food, playing with my kids, I'm going to put her to work and she's one of the back up singing on this new album. And what else is your godfather doing for you? Come on now don't be shy! God hasn't given you the spirit of fear."

"Oh my gosh," Shay blushed. "Producing."

"Producing what?" he asked.

"My first single and our duet," she smiled as the crowd went wild.

"You going to let them hear it?" Judah asked.

"A little bit," she giggled. "Wait my song or the one with the two of us?"

"I'll start," Judah laughed as he cued the band.

He sang with Shay for a minute, letting her take the lead as the spotlight closed in on her. He quickly rushed off stage, muted his mic and grabbed a bottle of water from an assistant. He smelled Derika's perfume before she touched his back, and he turned to see her standing with her arms, letting him know he pushed the limit.

"Strain your voice like that again, you're going to miss a tour date," Derika warned as he playfully hugged her. "You're just coming off of a bad cold and you said you were going to take it easy. Judah, please be careful."

"Dee, I'm good," he assured her. "I got to give them what they came for right?"

"You got four more cities," she reminded him as she unplugged her earpiece as an extra precaution. "If you need a track-"

"You know I don't ever do that," he said, turning back to look at the stage. "Music is too serious to fake on a stage, Dee. But look. Our baby is ready."

"She's not," Derika said. "She's still a little girl in so many ways. This industry is not for the faint of heart. And she's a teenage girl. Don't embarrass her with those long drawn out stories like that again. She has a lot of learning left."

"I taught her what I know, you teach her what you know," Judah said.

"Well I don't like the way your keyboard player keeps talking to her," Derika told him. "You need to deal with that before I have to put Ruby on him. You know the road is not the place for a wide-eyed girl. I told you one city backstage but now you've got her singing on stage. You're exposing her without properly training her. You are putting her in a position of being exposed too soon and the wrong people talking in her ear the second you look away."

"No one is stupid enough to try," Judah said. "Besides, we're in this together. Always."

"Always," she held his hand.

Judah leaned down to kiss her. She was average height but even in her heels, he towered over her. Together, they made an attractive couple who appeared supportive and rock-solid with each other. They were relationship goals for many and spent a lot of their time together as partners.

"You better stay in the spirit, mister," she pushed him back when she felt his hand sliding down her hip.

He winked at her and rushed back to the stage after unmuting his mic. Derika smiled as she shook her head and watched him prepare for another song. Certain cues he gave made her realize he was about to speak and ad-lib more than sing and let Ruby take it. Judah didn't always admit it, but he listened to her more than she realized he did.

"That man sure has some anointing in his voice!" a familiar voice startled Dericka.

She glanced over to see Moe Edwards, a pastor they knew beaming as he watched Judah. He turned to her and looked at her in a way that made her detest him.

"He is blessed indeed," she responded.

"He is blessed to have you," Moe told her. "The good book says that a man who finds a wife finds a good thing and obtaineth favor. And you, my dear, are worth more than rubies as a wife, as a mother, as a manager. I've known Judah since before he was born and he is truly obtaining favor. I never thought I'd see the day this stadium would sell out to a gospel singer. But here he is. Sold out within two hours of releasing tickets. I guess young people like that style of hippity-hop or R&B with that traditional blend. He is a soldier in the army of the Lord! And you, my dear, are his lieutenant!"

"All the glory belongs to the Lord," Derika nodded, making a mental note to ensure Moe was off the backstage list at future concerts.

"Tell me something," he leaned in. "The new singer Judah is mentoring. How old is she?"

"Our goddaughter?" Derika raised her eyebrows. "She's about fifteen to twenty-five depending on who the judge is. Judah is the only one who will be working with her for quite some time. I am personally managing her as well."

"Oh excuse me," he quickly looked into his phone. "I have to check something right quick."

"You go on and do that, Pastor," Derika walked away, satisfied she made the right decision to have Shay booked into the room with Ruby who she knew wasn't going to allow any room for idleness.

Derika had developed a knack for recognizing men of the cloth and men who used the cloth for personal gain. Moe was one of those who absolutely sought to gain the world, and was known to be wild on the road. Of course, these things were never discussed in public. Judah always trusted Derika's spirit of discerning things, especially seedy people and bad business. That was part of why he needed her present when big deals were being made.

When asked what it was about Judah that made her marry him, Derika was quick to say had she known he was an ordained pastor when they began dating, she would have ran the other direction. She was glad he was "just Judah" when they were together even though a visit to his family's church would be a reminder that he was very much respected as a pastor.

"That Judah sure has an anointing on him and the niece is very impressive," another man interrupted her thought. "I guess you've heard that a whole lot. That little exchange between you and him was sweet to see."

Derika initially ignored him and pretended to be busy on her phone. "Gospel people think it's about getting wings in heaven but I'm about living on earth like it is in heaven," the man puffed on a cigar. "Your husband has numbers out of this world. I took into account the work he does with secular artists. A lot of people would die if they knew he was writing and producing that stuff but I am sure you must be proud. Judah has a few signatures only a trained ear would recognize. By the way, I'm Pat Smith."

"The Pat Z. T. Smith?" Derika felt silly for not recognizing him. "You are a legend in the music industry!"

She should have known he wasn't average based on his simple yet expensive suit and jewelry. He was not over the top but had just enough to let one know that he was important.

"Your husband is a legend," Pat chuckled, shaking hands with her. "So legendary in fact I had to come see for myself who this man is that earned me millions off of my artists. That man is something special. But I don't have to tell you that. You're not one of those typical industry wives who sit home and reap rewards. You're obviously seeing it first hand. About your niece, is she sticking to gospel?"

"That's his goddaughter from Atlanta," Derika corrected him. "She's like our child. Her father and Judah were very close until he died. Judah stepped in to help her mother with her. We are both very protective of her."

"She is pretty," Pat remarked. "Right complexion, right hair texture, right height… easy marketability into mainstream. Of course, I don't have to tell you that would mean a full-time shift. Keep your eyes on her and have a chat with her sooner than later." Derika nodded.

"But that Judah," Pat puffed his cigar again. "He is the only person I know able to bounce between secular and gospel with ease. He's the first artist to have contributed to eight songs on the top ten charts at the same time. I want a piece of that. Can you make that happen or do I need to speak to another manager?"

"I am the one to speak to," Derika nodded. "I'm sure I could, for the right royalty cut and a few masters, sit down and have a chat."

"Oh you are smarter than I gave you credit for Mrs. Waters," Pat smiled. "I own masters. However, if you prepare that girl to be ready in about three to five years, I'll agree to her masters, but what I do with Judah I want those masters."

"Judah has hours of her already laid down and he will ensure she owns her work because that's what fathers do for daughters," Derika said. "If you want to talk to him, he will have a royalty cut of at least half, especially if he is writing and producing anonymously. I don't care how many lives you changed Pat, we are not impressed with making you richer. We live pretty comfortably and don't care for anything but ownership. I'm hearing masters, stocks and company shares or no meeting."

Pat seemed a bit shocked she was able to call his bluff so quickly and boldly.

"Some men choose a mind and some beauty, but some luck out and get both in the same woman, don't they?" Pat chuckled, impressed with her. "So I have to ask, are y'all more music industry folk or church industry folk?"

"What do you mean by that?" she asked.

Pat studied her for a moment, taking in her stance, her makeup, hair and dress. She prided herself with her natural breasts and thighs and had a confidence about her that made her more attractive than other women she was in rooms with. Pat saw it and without her responding, he seemed to have his answer.

"I've done my research," he said, reaching for her phone. "You two call me after the concert. There's some folks I'd like you to meet at my penthouse. Discretion is key of course but I am certain you two understand the importance of shall we say, closed-mouthed lions in the lion's den. And please get a babysitter. This is not a bring your kid to work meeting. One of those midnight soirees, then discuss matters over brunch things. If not, we can catch up if I have time when I get back to California."

Derika thought for two seconds of what Judah would want her to do, then gave Pat her phone and allowed him to type in his number. A few hours meeting after hours wouldn't hurt and it was always better to get the first opportunity.

"Is there anything in particular I should ensure is on the menu?" Pat asked.

"How about you wait for me to confirm if we're even attending?" Derika told him. "It was a pleasure Mr. Smith but I have to focus on the show."

"I'll see you in a few hours," he said confidently.

"If you're lucky," she told him, walking off knowing that he would watch her as she left.

CHAPTER 2

"We got to go," Judah woke up the next morning to Derika shaking him. "I let you sleep as long as I could."

He lazily opened his eyes and realized how much light was in the room. He sat up and looked out the window and noticed the view of a park and water in the distance and smiled thinking of how blessed they were.

"Yeah okay," he stretched in the bed before something on the nightstand caught his attention.

"No!" Derika said, snatching it from him. "You can have coffee."

"It was a gift Dee," he protested.

"I let you take a sample last night in front of the cool kids but you are not going to bring that back into our lives ever again," she told him. "Get dressed. And after brunch, I need to stop by the pharmacy for a pill."

"Did we?" he asked, lighting what was left of a joint.

"We did," she said.

Judah took a deep inhale to let the smoke flow through his nose and feel the sensation in his throat.

"I thought you wanted another baby," he glanced at her.

"Between you and JJ and Maya, I think my hands are full," she said, getting up to go to the bathroom. "Let's not forget a few other people like Shay and The Corner Stone and Mr. Cameron Diggs are all asking me to manage them."

"Tell Cameron Diggs you don't have time to manage an athlete," Judah stood in the bathroom doorway watching her empty the white dust from the trinket in the sink. "He's about to get traded anyway and you have help when it comes to me because I have other managers."

"And I have to manage them," Derika reminded him. "They all check me to make sure it's good for you. And you... Just remind me to stop to the pharmacy."

Judah put his arms around her and kissed her neck.

"Was it good though?" he whispered in her ear.

"I'm so sick of you," Derika laughed. "Get dressed. Pat wants us at brunch which will be in about twenty minutes."

"Are you wearing that?" Judah asked.

Derika looked at herself in the mirror and thought she was more than appropriate considering how quickly she packed them an overnight bag.

"Hair to the side, show a little neck," Judah spoke as he adjusted her. "It's real sexy like that. A little bit of skin goes a long way. Pull this skirt up from a calf-length to a peek of your knee. Lose this business blazer, unbutton this here, and add my belt around this blouse. Darker lips and boom. It's not church, Dee."

"According to your mother, I still dress too scandalous for church," she said looking at his changes and agreeing that it took her from professional to seductive.

"So what," Judah shrugged, pulling her closer to him. "You're my wife."

"According to her, I'm only your wife because I trapped you with JJ," Derika moved his hands and walked off to find her shoes. "She had someone better lined up for you just like she had Rachel lined up for Josiah. She loves JJ and Maya but she has called me a whore and bitch to my face more than once."

"You and my mom have got to stop all that shit," he sighed. "Remember how bad it was that first Thanksgiving you came home?"

Derika hated to even think of it. Lavinia Waters knew her sons were destined for greatness, being born into a church dynasty. Ministry was to be their mission in life. Like his older brother Josiah, Judah had been ordained a pastor in their church at an early age, charged with the music ministry. They won numerous awards but it was him leading or being a soloist that caught people's attention. Being in Atlanta, it took no time for someone to offer a record deal to Judah and he took it even though they struggled to define his sound. By the time he got to California, it was Derika, a young intern who noticed they were taking more than they should have been taking from him and advised him to come up with a plan to buy himself out and get a better deal elsewhere. She'd gotten a job at the label as an assistant and the two connected over a late night jam session. During their conversations, they realized she was the granddaughter Sis. Bradley had cared for during the summer, now all grown up. He had been to camp most of the time she visited but they found out they knew at least five mutual people from the church. He trusted she had his best interests and appointed her as his advisor then added her on the payroll as his lead manager. She also accepted his invitation to join him when he went home to get away from work for a minute and became fast friends with Josiah's wife Rachel.

"When the Lord sends you a helpmeet, you acknowledge it because that means he has sent you someone as he is preparing to take you to the next level," Bishop Darold Waters had told Judah after he observed they were together for a minute 'without labels'.

"We're just really good where we are and we are great friends," Judah had responded. "Mostly business stuff. You know how it is."

"I can't say I've seen you take an interest in many young women for more than a few weeks, but if you want my blessing, you've got it," Darold assured him. "If not, move out of her way and let the Lord send her the right man. Don't be blocking her blessings"

"I don't think she's his type," Josiah chuckled.

"Rachel wasn't your type until you found out that lawyer was talking to her," Darold reminded Josiah. "Played mind games with her for years but you came to your senses real quick when you saw them at dinner. I told you, going full-time into ministry, you needed a wife. Just like you about to blow up with your music Judah, you need a wife yourself."

"First of all, Daddy you know I was just trying to teach Rachel a lesson," Josiah said. "I had to reel her in correctly. There was an entire science to it."

"Fool please!" Judah laughed. "You were focused on her since you were ten. Had her pictures hidden in your drawer, staring at her every time she was in church. She had choices."

"I was her best and only choice," Josiah told them. "She was not going to find better than me."

"I have to admit you were sprung son," Darold agreed. "Crying like a baby to his own wedding before she even put her foot on the aisle. Bawled like a baby pulling back her veil. Hot mess."

"She was the prettiest bride ever to come through Greater Gates and still I'm happily, and I do mean kid in a candy store with free balloons, happily married while Judah is into himself," Josiah threw a worm at his brother. "He is not the marrying kind, Daddy. Going to be him and his music forever and he'll be okay with that."

"I see what I see," Darold said, turning to Judah. "Do something before someone else does. As for you, Josiah, you better have that sermon on lock, you here teasing your brother."

"Come on y'all this is supposed to be a fishing trip and y'all out here in me and Dee's situation," Judah groaned, picking up the worm and throwing it back. "And don't mess up my gear man."

"You out there in Hollywood where any old thing could creep up on you," Darold noted. "You already know I want you boys to make wise choices and your best thing to have is a woman who has your best interests as a priority. That girl has your back. Lock it down before you lose her. Watch my line. I need to go get that other can of bait. And don't think I ain't heard you say Dee not Derika."

Darold had barely walked off when Josiah leaned to Judah.

"He's right," Josiah told him quietly. "You should let her go if she is in no way prepared to handle what you got going on. However, if she is prepared, then keep her close because you know what's going to eventually happen at church. Whatever you have between the two of you, don't let Daddy dictate it and for sure as hell don't let Mama in at all."

Lavinia, or First Lady Waters as she preferred to be called, felt Derika was a golddigger and would be Judah's downfall, especially in gospel. She mandated her sons marry women with a bit more church pedigree. For four generations, her family birthed great names in ministry, earning a net worth of millions. Combined with Darold's books and speaking engagements, they had a life that included a large home in a prominent neighborhood, several luxury vehicles and commercial buildings. A busty woman in a tight dress with a music industry background was not ideal for her son.

"Satan comes in various forms even in the form of hips and thighs and lustful eyes," Lavinia grumbled in a corner when she heard Darold had introduced Derika as Judah's girlfriend in front of church people. "The nerve of him bringing her into our home, amongst our friends? And in that dress? Josiah, please talk some sense into your brother and stop letting them lay up in sin under your roof when they visit. You are a senior pastor now and should not be condoning that."

"Mama don't be like that," Josiah sighed. "You told him he better be married by thirty and now you're complaining that he keeps bringing a woman you don't like. I like her for him and Rachel likes her. She's really a sweet girl and very savvy too. Don't you want your son to be happy?"

"No," Lavinia shook her head. "Happiness is overrated and abiding by a standard is everything."

"Why y'all here in a corner?" Darold asked as he and Judah walked over to them.

"Judah, why can't you be like your brother and find a nice front pew-sitting, church event planning, women's ministry participating, wife?" Lavinia looked over to where Rachel and Derika were chatting together. "I can think of several praying for a man like you. You had to find yourself an industry Jezebel! Bringing her to my house in front of guests like that. She has probably been passed around more than an offering plate."

"Proverbs 15:1 reminds us that a soft answer turneth away wrath but grievous words stir up anger," Josiah put his hands on Judah's shoulders before he could respond to Lavinia.

"Pastor Waters, doesn't verse twenty say something about a wise son making a father glad but a foolish son despiseth his mother?" Lavinia asked sarcastically.

"Y'all go round the folks up to get to the table," Darold advised his sons before turning back to Lavinia. "That was uncalled for. We raised two exceptional young men who can make their own choices and you can't disrespect people like that. Behave yourself please."

A few minutes later, Lavinia glared at Judah and Derika whispering and giggling as they sat next to Josiah and Rachel at the table. Rachel saw the good in everything so of course she would have told Josiah she thought Derika was sweet. Lavinia drew claws when she felt her family under threat and would not let a woman like Derika gain access.

"Well, family and friends, Bishop is going to pray and then we can all eat!" she smiled at her guests as she glided across the formal dining room to hand her husband the carving knife. "And please forgive me for not remembering to put a dress code down on your invitations as I thought everything was implied. Hopefully next year the turkey will be the only thing with breasts and thighs on full display at the table. And y'all know I can make a mean sweet potato pie so let's dig on in!"

Derika felt the glances but smiled when she felt Judah lean over to kiss her forehead and hold her hand. As Darold broke the tension with joyful banter, Derika felt the judgment from Lavinia and decided that she was not built to fight the First Lady, even though the Waters men assured her that Lavinia was simply testing her and Rachel offered to help if she needed it.

Judah's schedule kept him from Atlanta for a while but a few months later, the family flew to California to surprise him by attending a major music awards ceremony where he had five nominations. Lavinia immediately noticed women's items in Judah's home and demanded an explanation especially since she was under the assumption that Derika was out of the picture since there was little discussion of her. Lavinia got an explanation a few hours later when they arrived at the red carpet.

"This has got to be the most exciting thing I've ever experienced!" Lavinia beamed as celebrities strolled by. "Movie stars and music stars and our Judah right here! To think we're about to walk the red carpet in Hollywood!"

"Okay, you're next," Derika poked her head in their holding area out of nowhere. "Oh! Everyone is here."

"Yes, we are," Lavinia forced a smile. "And you are here because?"

"Mama..." Josiah warned.

"That explains why they said you had ten guests," Derika said quietly to Judah. "I thought it was going to be band members. Well, come on with your entourage. They just announced you."

"Let's go then," Judah stepped out before the others.

"Me on a red carpet!" Lavinia smoothed her dress. "The whole of Atlanta is going to be talking!"

"You look wonderful!" Rachel assured her. "But maybe we ought to go on in and let Judah have his moment?"

"We *are* his moment as his support system," Lavinia told her. "Come on now."

"Mama... I think Judah wanted to talk to you earlier," Josiah began.

"Well he can tell me later because he knows I am not done with all that stuff around his place," she said, stepping out.

"Wait," a production assistant put up a hand to prevent her from joining Judah. "Them first."

"I am his mother!" Livinia protested.

"Dates get priority," the production assistant explained.

"Date?" Lavinia repeated looking over.

"Now, Lavinia -" Darold spoke up.

"What in the hell?" Lavinia gasped.

"Okay you can go now," the production assistant permitted them to join Judah.

Lavinia smiled for the cameras as she walked to Judah with the rest of the family behind her.

"I know you are not nominated for an urban gospel album award and out here with the evidence of your sin," she whispered to Judah while smiling through her teeth. "I am going to deal with you later."

The photographers took a few shots of them.

"Judah, can I get one with your hand on Derika's bump?" a photographer called to them.

"Of course," Judah smiled, touching Derika's visibly pregnant belly.

"Did you know?" Lavinia turned to Darold and Josiah.

"Yes," Darold said. "They got married at the courthouse and tomorrow they're having a ceremony for friends and family. That's the real reason we came and we didn't tell you because if you knew you wouldn't come."

Lavinia scowled through the ceremony and made it clear she was highly upset with all of them. She posed for photos, attempted to be amicable, but told Judah she would not speak to him again and told Darold and Josiah not to speak of them. However, when she walked in on Josiah and Darold celebrating with a box of cigars a few months later, Lavinia insisted on flying out to see her first grandchild and ensure Derika wouldn't do something stupid like go into postpartum depression and harm JJ.

As the years went by, Derika eventually learned to tolerate Lavinia who still had a lot to say. Lavinia was why Derika still second-guessed herself, just as she was doing in the present day in preparation for brunch.

"Do you know what she said to me during Josiah's ordination?" Derika asked Judah.

He came out of his daze and saw her directly in front of him.

"Who do you mean?" he asked, smoking a little more.

"All that I just said about how she treats me?" Derika sighed. "I mean your mother."

"Babe, I don't give a rat's ass about you and my mom, I really don't," Judah said, kissing her shoulder. "Wear the Chanel perfume."

"You're getting high off that shit that's what," Derika told him. "Put that thing down, take a shower and get dressed. And your father called this morning. Call him back because he has to talk to you about the Haiti mission."

"What are the kids up to?" Judah asked. "When is Rachel going to get them?"

"I didn't ask," she said. "Do we need to worry about them when they are with your parents?"

"Yes," Judah said. "I prefer when they are with Jo and Rachel."

"Well your parents raised you and for the most part, you're okay," Derika sat on the bed to put on her shoes. "We'll see them soon. Let's get a move on. It's not every day Patrick Smith invites people into his inner circle. After last night, we tore that door down and I am not letting you sign anything without reading it through at least three times."

Judah complied, realizing it was easier to just go with the flow.

"What else happened last night?" he asked, noticing a few adult novelties on the bed. "You packed all this, plus clothes? You are always prepared. Can we show up late?"

He tossed a small vibrator to her.

"Judah stop procrastinating when there is a one hundred million dollar breakfast on the line," Derika told him seriously. "And call your brother. He said he has something very important to discuss with you. Don't nobody have time to play around and be late to ruin a hell of a good deal."

"Yes ma'am," he chuckled as he went back into the bathroom, turned on the shower then went to the counter to brush his teeth first. "Dee... did you pack a toothbrush?"

She walked in and put it on the counter, then to his surprise, turned him to face her and lowered herself.

"Eleven minutes, and anything over is considered interrupting the itinerary," she said. "And put that out."

"Nah baby," he said, feeling himself grow within her mouth. "You blow, I blow. Damn... that's it right there."

He took a deep whiff and smiled as he felt it hit. He thought to himself just how blessed he was to have her.

CHAPTER 3

Derika enjoyed California mornings when she could sit near the pool and look at the gorgeous landscape in the distance. She loved their house that included their cars, her office space, Judah's studio and the comfortable lifestyle they worked hard for and returned to. The solace was short-lived when she went into the house and heard JJ and Maya yelling at each other. She almost regretted giving the housekeeper a week off but was so glad the tour was over so that they could live like a family. They had flown with Shay to Atlanta and returned to California with JJ and Maya.

"Hey hey!" she warned as she stepped inside. "Daddy is finishing up something in the studio and the last thing he needs is to hear you two on the track."

"Then why would he make the room soundproof?" JJ asked without looking up from his phone. "We're not stupid."

"You know what, you are too fast on your mouth little boy," Derika told him as she heard the piano in the other room. "Maya, I hope you are not messing with that piano after it was just tuned. Your daddy told you clean fingers not food fingers."

"See I washed my hands first," Maya said, skipping in. "We going on the plane with Daddy?"

"Not this time," she replied, clearing their dishes from the counter. "And you two are big enough to put your plates in the dishwasher. JJ, get off the phone please. No games today. And I know you have a project that is due next week so get on that."

"It's a family tree project but I can't finish it when my family is on a tour," he told her.

"Judah Waters, Jr, I am not getting into a debate with you today," Derika said firmly. "All you had to do was send me a text or call your grandmother. You are not going to blame us traveling for work, to give you the life you have become accustomed to as a reason for your project not being done."

"Well, why have kids if you don't take them places?" Maya asked climbing on a stool. "You took Shay."

"Daddy and I do not think the road is the place for a little kid," Derika explained. "Late nights, seedy people, uncomfortable buses and hardly any sleep. You'd miss school and your friends. And this trip to Haiti is not to go and have fun. Grandpa and Uncle Josiah are doing a lot of hard work feeding people, helping children who don't have parents and building the church. Daddy should have been gone two days ago but he had an important meeting."

"That meeting can't be that important if you not there," JJ shrugged.

Derika laughed as she ruffled his hair and thought how blessed they had been in the past nine years with their children. Maya was beautiful, outspoken, sweet and an absolute Daddy's girl. Judah had explained in an interview that the reason he showed up with his nails painted was that Maya had done them during their tea party and he was not going to take it off until she told him to. She was far more interested in music and had already appeared on a track with Judah. Meanwhile, JJ was already showing he might be a potential athlete. He was very social but at the same time, enjoyed his space. He enjoyed sitting in on sessions with Judah but was more interested in the technical aspect with no interest in performing.

"Can you do me a favor and let Daddy know we need to leave soon because of traffic?" Derika asked them as the house phone rang. "Then we can go by the pier. First one to tell him gets to choose where we eat."

As the children ran off to find Judah, she wondered who would be calling the house as it was a number they barely used.

"I am so sorry Derika!" the voice on the line cried when she answered.

"Is this you Ruby?" Derika asked. "What did you do to be sorry about? Are you leaving the band? You can't do this to us after all this time. We were supposed to talk about that management company together."

Ruby was one of the older band members who tried to ensure everyone stayed prayed up and things stayed scandal-free. She told Derika that Shay could bunk with her when she came on the road.

"Judah…" Ruby's voice cracked.

"What about Judah?" Derika raised an eye. "Girl what are you going on about?"

"Haiti…" she sniffled.

"He'll be there tomorrow," she told her. "We had a meeting with Pat Smith for that big deal that's coming down the pipeline he had to be here for."

"So he's home?" Ruby breathed a sigh of relief.

"Girl, what is going on with you calling me getting me all worked up?" Derika asked.

"Turn on the news," she said quickly. "It's all over the news. They said the whole orphanage and church done came down."

Derika quickly turned on the tv.

"Oh my God, Ruby is this real?" Derika put a hand over her heart as the images came across the screen.

"If you don't know that means he doesn't know," Ruby suddenly realized. "I'm going to come over right now. I'll be there soon."

Derika sat dumbfounded as she saw the devastating images, unsure of what emotion to let out first.

"Okay babe, I'm almost ready and the kids are putting on their clothes," Judah walked in a few minutes later. "You should hear that last mix. That shit is fire… Dee, you listening?"

Derika quickly blinked so he wouldn't see the initial look in her face.

"Judah… where are your phones?" asked Derika.

"Downstairs in the studio," he said. "I turned them off right after I talked to Josiah. He liked it. I'll get them when I go back down there. You know it is when you find the right flow."

"Babe… come here with me," Derika held out her hand for him to sit with her. "Right now."

"Dee, I'm only going for two weeks," he said sitting next to her. "You been crying? Miss me already?"

"We have to go to Atlanta," she cleared her throat quietly. "Paul Jones… Senior Pastor Jones confirmed it."

"What are you talking about?" Judah asked, confused.

Derika looked back to the television unsure of how to tell him that something unimaginable occurred. Judah followed her eyes just as photos of his father, brother and sister-in-law showed up with several other people.

"Turn that up," he told her.

"Judah wait," she began wanting to tell him before he saw it on the news.

He took the remote from her and turned up to volume.

"Shock waves are sweeping the gospel community now that Bishop Josiah Waters and his wife Rachel are confirmed to be among the dead Americans in this morning's earthquake," the journalist spoke. "His father, Bishop Darold Waters, who served as national overseer is still missing, presumed dead."

"Any word on Judah?" another journalist asked. "As you know, he is the member of the Waters family who is more well known especially just coming off his tour."

"Now we are told that he was scheduled to be here as this was a family and church project they have worked on in other parts of the world for years, the band, Judah 3:16 even donating some proceeds of music tours to fund it. We have made attempts to reach his team but nothing just yet. Now, we do know that Josiah and Rachel had been in the process of adopting a child from Haiti and opening another church and orphanage there. So learning that aspect absolutely makes this story even more tragic. Our hearts go out to the Waters family and Greater Gates Church community. As soon as we have an update on Judah 3:16 we'll let you know."

Judah sat frozen for a moment in disbelief as the house phone rang again. He felt Derika's arms around him as he lost all sense of what was going on and felt the tears fall. When he finally caught himself, he realized he was upstairs in the bedroom. He ventured downstairs and saw that Derika had already assembled assistants at the house, called for their part-time nanny to help, released a statement and had Pat Smith book them a jet. Ruby and a few other band members were there, assisting her where they could.

"Judah?" Ruby led him to a chair. "Come drink a glass of water now. We have everything under control. Derika is being Derika and she has everything under control. She had to give you a sedative and the fellas took you up to rest for a moment."

"I got to go to Haiti," Judah said, getting up. "I got to go get my brother."

"Derika!" Ruby called. "Derika I need you over here!"

Derika rushed over with two of the men.

"Judah, please don't make me call the doctor," Derika begged.

"I got to go get my brother," he said, pushing past her without realizing his strength and making her fall.

"Y'all better hold him," Ruby advised. "That sedative wore off too soon. Hurry up. We need him calm before the children get home."

As the men held him, Derika got up and pulled out a syringe and stuck Judah with it. Within a few moments, they saw it working and the men took him back upstairs.

"I'm not going to leave you by yourself tonight," Ruby whispered to Derika when she went into the bathroom to wash her face.

"Thank you…" Derika said. "You can take the guest on the first floor if you want."

"I may not sleep," Ruby said. "Derika how has he been lately?"

"He's good," Derika told her. "You know he's not there anymore."

"You need to call the doctor because you gave him too much," Ruby said. "Does he get aggressive with you when he's on that stuff?"

"He's fine," Derika assured her. "I don't need them holding him or testing his blood when we need to travel."

"Are you afraid of what they will find if they test him?" Ruby asked. "Is he sticking to his plan? Do we need to prepare for a situation?"

"Ruby please," Derika sighed. "I don't need any judgment from you."

"Derika, I'm not getting in your business but the amount you gave him would overdose the average person," Ruby said.

"He does not need to be institutionalized just because he is in mourning," Derika told her. "He'll be fine. Now please, I have to figure out how to get him to Atlanta and tell the children."

"Well," Ruby said. "I will be out there if you need me."

"I've got shit to do," Derika told her.

"You got to keep an eye on him before other eyes start noticing too," Ruby warned as she turned to leave. "I'm going to make sure everything is under control."

"Ruby…" Derika looked up. "He really doesn't mean to do anything but escape from himself. He doesn't hurt me. Not intentionally. That one time was a one-time thing."

"Well…" Ruby nodded remembering how scary that incident was. "I'm a friend and I care and you can call and know I'm here."

"I appreciate you being here," Derika continued. "Would you mind leading us in prayer? I know Judah normally does but…"

Ruby gave Derika a maternal hug and led her back to the group.

"Now, I need everybody to just stop for a moment," Ruby said. "As an extended family, we need to lift Judah and Derika in prayer right now. We do not question God, because he knows best but it's praying time. So we are going to sing a little bit and pray a little bit and ask for a hedge of protection for Judah and Derika and the children as they journey in the midst of this tragedy."

As Ruby led a worship song, she held Derika close. Derika stayed with them until the children came home and assumed there was another jam session going on. They kissed their mother goodnight and went off to bed. As their friends prayed and sang, Derika snuck away to her bedroom where she found Judah looking drowsy.

"Hey Dee," he said quietly.

"Hey babe," she said as she climbed into bed beside him and placed his head on her shoulder. "Go back to sleep. When you wake up, we have stuff to do, okay?"

"Okay," he said.

By the time he was good enough to fly, Judah sat quietly even though the children were excited to have the whole plane to themselves. Derika took them to the seats away from Judah so they wouldn't disturb him. He only interacted with the children when Derika told them what happened. He admired how she was able to tell them the truth in a way they could understand but also give them comfort as they cried. It was odd to arrive and not have Rachel or Josiah pick them up and even more strange pulling up to the Waters family estate to see so many reporters lined up outside the gate. They all hesitated for a moment, thinking the same thing - that it just didn't feel like home without Darold bursting through the large front doors and asking where his grandbabies were.

As they entered the lavish home, several senior members of the church were gathered and quickly expressed condolences as they walked in. Judah made it a point to say thank you to all of them and then waited on Derika to settle the children in the kitchen with Anna, the chef before going to find his mother.

"They're with the Lord now," Lavinia said when they found her sitting in her bedroom holding a bible, dressed in her timeless classical style. "Josiah tried to shield them... the children and Rachel. She was reading to them. The whole wall came down on them. Rachel was still holding the baby. She'd named her Hope."

Lavinia looked at her phone and hit play on a video.

"Say hello to your grandmother, Hope," Rachel encouraged the baby in English then French in the video she recorded earlier that day. "Mama, I can't wait for you to hold her. And it's going to be soon now that we have her documents and passport. Say bye-bye to your grandmother, Hope! I'm going to send a video later when Judah's flight lands. Love you!"

"She had her in her arms, holding her tight," Lavinia seemed dehydrated from crying. "Josiah was on top of them and the children. Over eight hundred dead in that area so far, at least sixty dead in that building they were in. How your daddy managed to survive -"

"Bishop is alive?" Derika asked.

"Yes..." Lavinia said. "I am not a widow. They're bringing him home now. Pastor Jones was trying to bring Rachel and Josiah home but he was so busy with your father that by the time he got back, they took the remains away. Something about Haitians burying their dead quickly. They wasn't no Haitians. They were Americans. My poor child and his family buried in some mass grave without any dignity. Can you imagine? Rachel... such a beautiful girl. They told me she was unrecognizable. He identified her by her wedding ring and clothes. Rachel and Josiah likely burned and buried in a mass grave!"

"With the people and children they cared for," Dericka said gently. "They loved the Haiti mission and the people loved them."

"You never know what to say do you?" Lavinia glared at Derika. "I don't have nothing to bury here on our family plot and you are talking about them caring? He deserved to be resting with our family so I can go and see him. You expect me to go fly out there on his birthday or Christmas and Mother's Day to leave flowers? This is why I wanted Judah to come alone. Rachel always knew what to say. She was perfect and beautiful and righteous. God always takes the best and leaves others to provoke us from entering the kingdom."

"You're still here," Derika turned her head.

Judah gave her a look that let her know that he wanted her to try to stay. She pointed at Lavinia to remind him that she wanted to stay in a hotel instead of the family home without Darold.

"I'm here now, and we'll stay for as long as we need to," Judah embraced his mother.

"Thank you, son," Lavinia said before sobbing. "There is just so much to be done."

"Would you like for me to help with anything?" Derika offered. "I can call up some of our friends and get a memorial concert together for Friday."

"A concert at a time like this?" Lavinia shook her head. "It's all about industry with you. We are in mourning!"

"Josiah was a spiritual advisor to a lot of people in the industry including us," Derika shot back. "He deserves to be honored."

"Why didn't you honor him when he was alive?" Lavinia asked.

"Judah…" Derika looked at her husband.

"Mama, Derika is really good at arranging things on short notice," Judah said. "I would like to pay tribute to my brother and that's the only way I know how."

"Well, why didn't you say so, baby?" Lavinia touched his cheek. "Maybe we, as a family need to have a quick chat in private."

She looked at Derika, indicating she wanted her to leave.

"I am so sorry for your loss, Lavinia," Derika hugged her, then kissed Judah before she left.

"Y'all two need to stop," Judah told his mother. "We are here to help and to grieve together. I am not going to spend this time being a referee. Josiah was the peacemaker and I was the psalmist. I would like for you to please respect my wife."

"I can't make no promises," Lavinia said, inviting him to sit with her. "I have to speak to you, son. With your father injured and your brother gone, we are a headless church. That's why the elders have gathered so we can have somebody in place by Sunday. They suggested Deacon Nick Prescott or Pastor Paul Jones, but you too are a pastor and this is your family. You need to sit in on a board meeting and we have some decisions to make. I will not have this ministry my father and your father's father worked so hard to build to watch it be put asunder over this. We still lead even in the midst of tragedy."

Judah was amazed his mother was so focused on ensuring the church would continue over the immense loss they were dealing with. He was still dwelling on the last communication he had with his brother and still shocked over the whole situation. But here was Lavinia, already dressed in a black dress making sure the organizations the church was a part of did not step in to gain control.

"What exactly is Daddy's condition?" Judah asked.

"He lost a leg and internal injuries," Lavinia began sobbing. "He was talking when they pulled him out but went out when they were flying him over. We don't know if he will make it and I will never have closure with Josiah and Rachel and that precious baby."

"Oh Mama," Judah held her as they mourned together.

"Be a big boy and help Mama with some stuff now," Lavinia caught herself. "I need you to lead us in prayer and then we need to go on to the church and begin the vigil. And please tell your wife to change her clothes. Who mourns with tight pants and titties out? She has no respect for the church or for you."

"We barely had time to pack," Judah explained. "A new business associate got us here on his jet. We were so focused on getting here quickly we didn't care to look appropriate."

"Well now that you are here, do better," Lavinia advised standing. "It's just the two of us for right now. We have to trust in the Lord and let him have his way."

"I'm having the memorial concert," Judah said. "It can serve as a fundraiser for the other families affected and those on the ground. And I want Derika to handle it. She knows what I would say. I can't be two places at once so while I am dealing with this, she needs to act on my behalf."

Lavinia sighed. She was not in the mood to argue with Judah so she simply nodded.

After meeting with the guests, Judah got a call from the hospital regarding Darold and opted to rush there instead of the church. He was given a full report of what happened and the extent of his father's injuries. Judah insisted on staying the night in case his condition changed and advised Derika to contact Alphonso, the church's choir director to make sure his teams were prepared for the concert. Derika initially objected, telling Judah she would stay with him.

"She irritates me," Lavinia told Paul. "Please talk to Judah and tell him I cannot get into the right frame to pray with her hovering over him. He is not listening to me. Then you and I need to have a talk about Sunday. Get rid of her now!"

CHAPTER 4

"That old bitch is the one who should've died, not Rachel or Josiah!" Derika growled as she took another shot at Alphonso's house later that night. "That Paul dude with his big and tall self had no right suggesting I meet with you now while you are likely awake instead of wait til tomorrow. That translates to get your ass up on out of here."

Alphonso Dorsey was the first person Judah introduced her to in the church. A fashion designer and former entertainer, Alphonso was credited as the one who discovered Judah's talent and cultivated it. When he realized Judah wasn't able to read music, he patiently worked with him so that he could learn what everything sounded like. Over the years, Derika had also developed a friendship with Alphonso and he became the only person at the church aside from Darold, Josiah and Rachel with whom she could let her guard down.

"She might be mean but she did lose her favorite son and her husband is about dead too," Alphonso said. "Let this one slide."

"You do realize that had Judah not stayed for the meeting he would've been right there with them?" Derika reminded him. "She acts as if I am not hurt by this loss too. Rachel was like a sister and Josiah... I don't know how we made it this far without Josiah. I still wish she were the one who died, I swear I do."

Alphonso sipped his tea and watched her pace the floor in his brightly-colored French-inspired, fresh-bouquet-smelling home. Out of nowhere, he let out a hoot. Derika realized how silly she must have looked.

"Girl, you need to slow down and let's focus on this list of guests and singers," Alphonso laughed. "Don't get me wrong, I love hearing designer heels across my floors but baby, you are one messy drunk if ever I saw one, child. Come sit down."

"And you are just a hot damn mess," she chuckled. "Ooh, I had to get up out of that hospital from around her!"

"Well, you ain't going to be able to drive home tonight," he said, gesturing for her to sit down. "Now, I can get the choir on board and we can wear shades of gray. Do you need me to get some backup singers? Is this going to be on live tv or what? Because if it is, I need to pull out an Alphonso original with silk."

"It looks like it will be streaming live," Derika ran her fingers through her hair.

"Will Judah 3:16 be ministering in song or is Judah giving the eulogy?" he made notes.

"The band is coming but you know Judah," she said. "He'll likely do one of those eastern gates, when I get to Heaven, well done my servant, I got my reward, afterlife medleys. Maybe some negro spiritual. Judah says he goes where the spirit leads him and I just mind my business and signal to him when it's time to wind it down."

"That man has the most amazing anointing in his voice," Alphonso sighed. "I like that Ruby lady who sings too. Now she needs a solo album. I remember when I told Bishop to let him sing when he was knee-high to a grasshopper, with the mic bigger than him. Bishop was skeptical but that first note, oooh, it hits you like mmmm! Those Waters boys were a whole headache back in the day. Josiah was sly and slick. If he didn't become a minister, he might've become a pimp. But everyone loved Judah more because he was so approachable. That boy's first love was music and being on a stage. I cut his mic a couple of times he tried taking over my choir. I was so happy when he told me he got offered a record deal. He wasn't going to take it at first but I encouraged him to get up out of this city and explore a bit. And now look."

"Yeah well, he's still exploring," Derika said, drinking another shot.

"No ma'am," Alphonso took the bottle from her. "You are not going to have no confessional."

"I can confess with you though," Derika said. "You of all people know what it's like to show one face to the church and live your other face in private."

Alphonso flipped his shawl over his shoulder and leaned towards her. It was no secret that he was flamboyant and had a large personality he had taken on stage during the height of his drag queen days. Closer to sixty than fifty, he dedicated himself to the church after being born again. Single by choice, church people were comfortable with him.

"Girl, the church needs gays," Alphonso told Derika. "It's a prison to be a black gay man in a church but these days is so much easier than when we were out on the west coast. Nowadays, a lot of churches do marry and allow families in, but back then when you know who with all saints and sinners in his boudoir was up and about, girl it was not a thing to even whisper. Do you know any gays in church other than me?"

"None as open and bold and brazen as you," Derika told him. "Greater Gates is not a modern church so you and I know none will ever be accepted. Lavinia keeps it so traditional. But you're the only one I know who lives his truth, Alphonso."

"God is my all and all!" Alphonso raised a hand to heaven and shook his head. "Quiet as it's kept, a sissy in the sanctuary always brightens the day. You think they could survive without me leading the decorations team for special events or designing couture gowns? Honey, Alphonso has seven streams, so my tithes keep a lot of things running. Other churches have choir directors presenting a set, Greater Gates with choir director Alphonso, delivers an experience. So whatever you and your husband got going on, you need to have and hold, sickness and health, secrets and lies, that together. You hear me? Didn't nobody tell you to get involved with a music ministry man. Satan led the choir in heaven before he got kicked out and ever since then, it's a known fact that's where a lot of trouble in church starts. Been it and seen it."

Derika nodded and attempted to laugh.

"I don't know what it is you may be hinting at but I mind my business," Alphonso added. "For instance, it's not my business to tell you to tell him to stop rubbing his nose on stage. That monkey on his back is going to start throwing bananas."

"So you do know?" Derika looked up at Alphonso.

"I'm a second father to that boy and of course I know because I have been there in my past too," Alphonso sighed, pouring himself more tea. "I can tell you love him more than you love yourself, too. That is dangerous, child. Never love someone so much that you let that love blind you from the sin that others see. I'm so disappointed he's still dealing with it. I remember when he was about twenty or so, Bishop had asked me if I knew of any crack houses I thought Judah might be in on those days he'd go missing. By the time you met him, he was in a real good spot but of course, it came back. You are a strong woman to have stayed with him through rehab. Between you and me, Lavinia should be grateful to you for staying through that."

"Where was I going to go with a newborn and a toddler?" Derika lowered her head.

"My generation created that foolishness," Alphonso sighed again. "Nearly wiped most of us out. Between that and AIDS. It isn't obvious to an outsider but the way he has all that energy… that's a high that doesn't come from the Lord. That is his cross to bear. Just like that bottle is yours. You hide better because you're so busy protecting him. Baby, if you need an ally, I am here. I know you relied on his brother to help keep him together. If you want to, suggest that he speak to Pastor Paul Jones. He is very trustworthy and one of the few saints left that's why Bishop Darold kept him close. Bishop Darold had some secrets too. There is a reason why Pastor Jones accompanied him everywhere. Someone had to be there to make sure he stayed in check. Now, Bishop Josiah was the real deal but I think he left this world knowing he left his brother in good hands. My Lord, what a loss. Such a bright future and that poor little baby… How are you in all of this?"

Derika covered her eyes and her whole body began shaking as she started to cry. She realized that no one had asked her how she felt about the tragedy. Alphonso wrapped his arms around her and began humming as she reflected on her moments with Rachel who told her how God saw it fit to connect them all as family.

Rachel was the perfect wife and perfect listener. She offered Derika advice on how to speak loud by being silent and letting actions set the pace. The trips to Atlanta were so much more bearable when Rachel was there to help her along the way. She would miss the vacations they took together, when they left the titles and careers behind and were just a pair of brothers with their wives disconnected from responsibilities for a week. The trip the year Maya was born was a fun one as they rented a beachfront Caribbean home and boat.

"Look at them on those jet skis!" Derika had sat up to watch Judah and Josiah play on the water. "Acting like a pair of children out there."

"They're just showing off for us," Rachel looked up from the book she was writing. "Just bring it up at dinner, tell them it looked so dangerous and make them think they did a thing. You know men love impressing women, even if they are married to them."

"You are so unimpressed," Derika sat back down in her deck chair and sipped her drink. "I ordered this rum punch with more rum than punch and I'm still sober. Don't get me wrong, I love my babies but I couldn't wait to get away and be grown. Maya is so clingy and miserable. Only thing that gets her to sleep is Judah playing that piano or singing to her while she's on his chest. I hope she's giving Lavinia headaches and throwing tantrums. Why are you not getting drunk? You waiting for Jesus to turn water into wine?"

"I am not a big drinker so please feel free to have my share," Rachel smiled at her before looking back at their husbands. "Josiah and Judah are different as day and night but isn't it amazing that they have that love for each other? And the best part is we get to be the lucky ladies who get to be the extension of them."

"Easy for you to say when Lavinia handpicked you from the lineup of virgins for her precious firstborn son," Derika sighed. "She feels I trapped Judah."

"But you kinda did," Rachel shrugged. "We all trap our men because we decide when they can get us. But you got to know him, he got to know you, you built an amazing friendship and now here you are business partners, lovers, parents and it was your choice to be together. And for the record, don't act like you don't know preacher's kids are the ones furthest from heaven. I assure you, Lavinia did not pick a virgin."

Derika nearly choked on her drink, shocked that Rachel was not as perfect as she appeared to be. They knew people compared them to each other and it never bothered them because they got along just fine. Josiah and Rachel were more by the book and traditional while Judah and Derika were more outgoing and flashy. Rachel was modest, wearing coverups on the beach while Derika had no issues wearing the fashion-forward and revealing swimsuits Judah chose for her.

"Are you serious?" Derika chuckled. "Oh! The way she speaks of your virtue, I thought you took that thing right to your marriage bed in your white wedding princess gown."

"Girl please," Rachel sipped a little wine. "If it's one thing Lavinia did is birth two fine, tall, chocolate specimens. Of course, I think I got the sexier one, but that's just me. Just look at him. You think I was going to let that pass me by? I fell hook, line and sinker with that son of a preacher man kind of thing that Queen Aretha used to sing about. Literally every time Darold preached at my daddy's church and they came along, Josiah had something slick to say to me. Well, one day I answered him back and he answered me back and we went for a walk arguing along the way and before we got back to the porch, he kissed me. Like a grown-up, held me close, like he knew what he was doing kiss."

"Oh my gosh, that is too cute!" Derika burst out laughing.

"That was cute little puppy love," Rachel sighed. "A couple years later, that was an all-out situation and we got ourselves right into trouble."

"Really now?" Derika raised her eyes. "What could two kids do?"

"Girl, me and Josiah were messing around since vacation bible camp days, right before chapel in the morning and just after lights out at night," Rachel confessed. "No one seemed to notice and we were good at sneaking around even at church events. I had my mother fooled thinking I wasn't even holding hands with him but if those church walls and garage and basement could talk. Busy parents mean less eyes watching. Judah was so quiet and sweet back then but Josiah… all the girls wanted him, and he was so fast he probably got quite a few of them too. We weren't supposed to be dating like that but people always said we were so cute together. Then we drifted apart when he went off to school, but my mother and his mother made sure I was present when he returned from bible college because a newly ordained pastor had better be married or engaged. I just let him chase me for a while to think I wasn't interested. When you think about it, I had him before Lavinia decided I was right for him. Don't get it twisted. You saw us on the dance floor last night. I think I ended up with the wild one. Funny how wine makes you say a lot, doesn't it?"

Derika was always intrigued when Judah, Josiah and Rachel talked about their childhood growing up in church. It was a life she could not imagine and one she never desired. Judah told her she never had to worry about that because he wasn't even interested in reliving it.

"I envy you because you got the brother who can have fun and do what he is most passionate about in comfortable sneakers, jeans, and get to hype people every time he opens his mouth," Rachel said wistfully. "He can go on social media and show off his tattoos, harmonize with some of the world's biggest musicians and don't think I don't see how he gets you your cute outfits and dresses you up like you're his personal doll. He's confident in himself and loves to see you showing off your body. I can't be too expensive or dress too sexy because they will judge me and judge my husband's leadership. If a man can't lead a wife and children, he can't lead a church. That's the rule of thumb. Between all their investments, books, and music money, our future great-grandchildren are set, yet Josiah and I can't be flashy. You and Judah can rock your brands without judgment."

"It's a job," Derika told her as they both gazed at Judah and Josiah playing on the water. "You don't create Judah 3:16 overnight. You see how he can be in that creative zone. You and I would never think to add dancehall or rock or house/techno to traditional and urban gospel sounds. The stuff he does for other people is just unreal. And if I'm in a deep sleep he will still bring me down to the studio to ask if something sounds right or to help him. I have to admit, I really like that mad scientist genius in there. I'm just glad to let him do his thing so I can focus on running the businesses."

"I would lose my mind doing what you two do," Rachel laughed. "I love a routine. I love cooking and helping out and doing the work of the Lord. It's not for everyone but I really do love it and Josiah loves it. I feel like we are walking in our purpose. By the way, I want you to speak at the women's conference this year to talk about the life of a gospel music industry wife."

"Lavinia will never let me speak at anything the church hosts and I'm going to be honest with you, I'm not a Proverbs woman," Derika admitted. "Look at me, Rachel. I'm not the right person to speak at a church women's event."

"Lavinia is not God," Rachel reminded her. "I'm head of the women's ministry. We've had reality stars, actresses, convicted felons… relatable people not already polished people. You are going to be there and your story is going to change lives."

"They are not ready to hear my story," Derika said, taking a long inhale of the joint Judah left lit on her table. "I have a lot of things in my life that will have people judging me and making them think Judah is a damn fool. My grandmother gave so much of herself to the church and in the end, me and my aunt were the ones who had to pay for her final days in comfort."

"We all have a past," Rachel shrugged. "I thought I would be judged for the rest of my life for getting pregnant at fourteen."

Derika looked up at Rachel, startled by what she just said. Rachel turned to her.

"You were…" Derika couldn't get the words out.

"Judah didn't tell you?" Rachel seemed surprised. "I suppose he felt that it was my place to share if I wanted to, but I thought he would've told you. We got caught and got scared and dealt with it. It was right after Jo got his driver's license and I got a fake ID. We went out of state. The first time I told my story, someone in the room decided to keep the baby she was about to abort and now that little one is my godbaby. The second time I told it, someone wanted to partner with me to help teen mothers. The third time, Josiah was with me and he actually spoke up and admitted that he was scared and felt we had let our parents down so he convinced me it was best. Then a boy told him he was sixteen and had a baby on the way and that opened up another ministry where men taught boys how to become fathers."

Rachel looked at Josiah and smiled.

"The thing is, we didn't think anything of it back then," she continued. "Didn't think we would end up married. And now we are married and can't seem to stay pregnant long enough. I already told Josiah he can go on ahead and have a baby and I'll even raise it. The first issue is since we were engaged, we haven't once been with anyone else. The second issue is he's still grieving. The last time we were pregnant was the last time. I can't do it again and he couldn't take seeing it was an actual baby that time. I wish I had just kept it the first time. Maybe God is punishing us. But the joke is on him because me and Jo still chose each other and we'll just have to find another baby. I know I am leaving this earth a mother."

"Does Lavinia know this?" asked Derika dumbfounded.

"She will know the whole thing when I publish this book I've been editing for over ten years," Rachel laughed. "The crazy thing is my cousin who lived with us had a baby at fifteen and my parents supported her and told her it was okay. Then I told them and they said had I come to them, they would've been there to help regardless of Lavinia. And Darold had told us he would've made Josiah do the right thing and he wishes we had spoken up and gotten help. Lavinia either has not been told or figured since we spoke about it after we got married she doesn't need to say anything. You know how much pressure church can be especially when your family is the one at the forefront. What's done in the dark always comes to light. See, what you think is your fire can be your freedom, what you think is a trial is your triumph, and your test is really your testimony. So even in your state of imperfection, God thinks you are perfect enough to make an impact. And you know what, I have to agree. You are fine just as you are, sis. We all have stories, testimonies and ways in which we overcome. I don't know what your story is as you didn't know mine, but I can tell you, we are in an exclusive club that has more liabilities than benefits. But I got you, just like the two of them over there acting like they're twelve on the water have each other."

Derika had tears in her eyes as Rachel hugged her.

"Here I am, liquor setting in, a little high and you're ministering to me," Derika started laughing.

"That's what sisters are for," Rachel wiped her eyes. "Now how about we go down there and give them a real reason to show off?"

Derika's phone rang and brought her back to the present where she found comfort in Alphonso's arms. As Alphonso continued humming, Derika realized she too lost a sibling and in that moment, she mourned Rachel.

CHAPTER 5

Judah watched Derika braid Maya's hair and kiss her forehead. Their chatter, the sun peeking through the bedroom window and pure joy in the moment brought him from a place of sorrow. Derika felt him looking at her and winked at him. He smiled for the first time in what felt like an eternity.

The past three weeks were extremely rough but somehow Derika managed to keep it together. The children were happy, she organized all that Judah needed then briefed him later and she found ways to not get in Lavinia's way. She even helped Rachel's parents when they wanted to get some of her things and suggested both families keep the house since the mortgage was paid off. With no heirs and no will, Judah found himself having to speak to attorneys to make sense of what to do.

The memorial service was a concert extravaganza bringing together some big names in the church world to pay their respects. Ruby took over the band and Alphonso the choir, both knowing the Derika style of doing things so she could focus on her family. Judah flawlessly led everything and everyone agreed it was the perfect sendoff. Everyone commended his strength and ability to carry everything so well. No one saw when he left the stage and went into what used to be Josiah's office, fell to the floor and bawled in Derika's arms. Against her better judgment, she gave Judah something to calm him down as Alphonso kept things going. Judah had another breakdown when they attended another memorial at Rachel's family's church but managed to get through the final one at Greater Gates. He tried his best to get through the grief and was grateful for her help.

"Am I pretty, Daddy?" Maya interrupted his thoughts as she jumped on his lap.

"You are God's creation, of course, you are beautiful," he told her. "You are also Mommy and Daddy's creation so yes, princess, you are truly a beauty. Don't grow up on me too fast."

"I won't!" she hugged him and giggled when he kissed her cheeks. "Ooh Daddy! Your beard tickles! You gotta shave that!"

"Go see what Ms. Anna is baking you lil' talkative thing," Judah laughed at Maya's bluntness. "It smells real good. And do not harass your brother."

Maya ran off singing to herself. Judah looked at Derika as she gathered the hair products.

"Mommy is beautiful too," he said, making her look his way.

"Is that the Judah I've been waiting to return?" she asked, sitting on his lap.

"I think so," he said, putting his arms around her. "You wash your hair with fruit salad? Coconut? Peach? Pomegranate?"

"If you don't stop!" Derika giggled. "And yes! Maya is right about you needing to shave. You haven't shaved since we were here. You excited we get to go home this week? Our own house, our own bed, your studio, the pool… I have one more bag to pack for each of us and then that's it. I am actually looking forward to hearing you in the middle of the night on the piano."

Judah brushed her hair from her face and looked into her eyes. He took a deep breath and she caught on to his silent communication.

"Hell no!" she said.

"Baby…" he began as she pulled away from him. "You don't even know what I'm about to say."

"You tell her you have a family and we have a life!" Derika pointed in his chest.

"Dee -" he began.

"Don't you Dee me!" she said as he quickly closed the door. "What did you do?"

"You going to calm down?" he asked.

"I am calm!" she put her hands akimbo and paced back and forth.

"Only until Daddy gets better -" Judah began.

"Get better?" Derika stopped and looked at him. "Crushed pelvis, severed leg, brain damage and can't breathe on his own. Your daddy is dead without those machines Judah. I thought you were waiting here to decide to pull the plug now that you have power of attorney."

"I am not killing my father," Judah shook his head. "Until God tells me otherwise, I will continue to pray for a miracle."

"The miracle needs to be you and me and the children on the flight by the end of the week going home," Derika told him.

"We are not leaving this week because I have to be at church on Sunday," Judah took her hands.

She took a deep breath and looked him in the eyes. She couldn't tell what he was going to say but anticipated she was not going to be happy.

"Out with it already!" she demanded.

"Effective immediately, I have been appointed Interim-Bishop of Greater Gates," Judah began as Derika shook her head in disbelief. "We will stay here for a while to help the church through this time."

"I am your wife and your manager and you didn't think to consult me?" she pulled her hands back. "You insist on me being at every important meeting to help you with your decision and you do this to me? Do you know how that makes me feel Judah?"

"Derika, it was just a meeting that I didn't realize was a board meeting," he said. "I thought I was going in with Mama and Pastor Jones. They all agreed that it would be best."

"We have a concert next week and you're headlining an eight-city tour next month," she reminded him. "Ruby's been busting her ass to practice the band and do interviews. She even sang your parts on that morning show last week. They are ready for you to come back. And Pat..."

"I have to cancel, Dee," he said.

"Judah!" she cried.

"I am minding my father's business," he said. "My earthly and my heavenly father."

"Judah you can't just go from a singer to an interim bishop," Derika shook her head. "Make it make sense!"

"The technicality is I have been ordained a youth pastor and have served as minister of music," he said. "Dee... I need you to be there with me on Sunday when they present me officially before the church."

"I need you in New York next month on that stage and in Hollywood next week as a judge on the tv show," she reminded him.

Judah watched her walk about the room and waited for her to calm down.

"The audacity of you even going to that meeting without telling me and then agreeing to this is so fucking disrespectful!" she walked up to him. "What the hell were you thinking? You didn't damn think! My anxiety is through the roof here and Maya is a bit hyper."

"Do you need more oil?" he offered her a small bottle.

"Yes, please let your mother know I'm giving the children marijuana so she can accuse me of drugging them," Derika rolled her eyes.

"Derika, we are all going to have to do things we don't want for the greater good," Judah said firmly. "Stop being selfish and get with it. Alphonso is stopping by to get us fitted for Sunday. I've also taken the liberty of picking out some clothes for you to refresh your wardrobe."

"You are the one who liked seeing me in what I have, mister raise up the skirt and lower the shirts," she seemed confused.

"Well now, you need to dress like the first lady of the church on Sunday and a dignified lady at other times," he said. "I have to change a bit too to fit in with what has been set."

"Since we are going to be here I need an SUV," she challenged him.

He took a step back and then walked to the door. He stopped and looked back at her.

"Leather interior with a sunroof?" he asked. "Have them run my credit and put the papers in your name."

Derika pushed the door shut and allowed herself to slide to the floor. She waited for a moment to see if he would come back and apologize to her. One minute went by. Then another. She realized ten minutes had gone by and he did not return. She felt as if he took away a part of her and worse, the part he helped create.

CHAPTER 6

"We are supposed to be shopping for accessories," Alphonso whispered to Derika the next day as she led them through an aisle at an adult store. "I am not a young man. I don't even know what half of these things are supposed to be for."

"I'm trying to make up with my husband," Derika told him. "I can't stay mad with him especially after that new SUV. I'm booking us a hotel and hopefully, we will both be relaxed enough on Saturday for the dinner and service on Sunday."

"Y'all young people can't just make love the old-fashioned way can you?" asked Alphonso. "All you need is two willing bodies, or in my case, one hand that don't have arthritis."

Derika lowered her sunglasses as she inspected the items. The store wasn't tacky and run down but rather professional and well-stocked. As Alphonso tried his best to remain discreet, Derika conversed with a staff member and tested products by turning them on to see their speeds and actions. She picked up a strap on and compared it to a ribbed dildo wondering aloud which might provide sensation to both partners.

"Why would a man need a strap on?" asked Alphonso quietly.

"It's actually a hollow," Derika explained. "See. He can put his thing inside and this just acts like an enhancer. It's not uncommon for couples with erectile dysfunction or the receiver wanting to feel something bigger than what their partner has."

"I shouldn't have asked," Alphonso closed his eyes. "This is why I stay single and mind my business. This is too much! Put this mess down and let's go to the other store to find you some gloves and earrings."

"I'm getting these items," Derika said. "I need a stress reliever and honestly, so does he. All of our things are at our own house... our beautiful house with a pool and three-car garage, mountain views and my office and Judah's studio. Sitting empty."

"Will the children be going to school?" Alphonso asked.

"Yes," Derika said. "Lavina enrolled them in some uppity private school. I can't stand her sadity ass."

"Derika," Alphonso put a hand on her shoulder. "Sweetie, you are about to be on full display. You can't be mad at Judah for stepping up and being honorable. You need to support him. He is going to need you, not these knick-knacks and most certainly not your attitude. He is going to go through some changes and pressures and you need to get out of this funk and be nice. Book your hotel, but talk to him. Let him know you respect him as a man so that he can walk into that building knowing at least one person knows him and will be there unconditionally. He ain't singing. He has a sermon to prepare. He needs you."

By the time Judah came in that night, the children were asleep and Lavinia was in her bedroom. He stopped in his father's office for a moment and put on some music to try to clear his head. He was grateful for Paul showing him the ropes but he was still concerned about his father's wellbeing. He also wondered what he was getting his family into. He played it safe by spending the night on his father's leather sofa to avoid whatever mood Derika was in.

Derika had always been the kind of friend he could share everything with and not be judged. She needed something to make her feel needed and he needed someone to keep him together. Their dynamic was one where trust and friendship outweighed intimacy and flaws. He knew he messed up in not bringing her into the conversation early on and the confusion that was setting in told him he needed her to help clear his thoughts.

He looked at his bible for a moment worried about Sunday. This was not his lane at all. He tried writing words and started humming to himself, eventually getting into composer mode.

"I can't do this, Jo!" he said aloud as if he were speaking to his brother. "I'm not supposed to do this. You were supposed to be here. I don't know what kind of God you served, sees you doing everything right, helping his people and takes you out in the prime of it."

Judah sat at the desk and picked up his father's bible for a moment. He tried reading it but got distracted by a toy JJ had left. He sighed and decided the best thing to do would be to apologize to Derika for his hasty decision and hope she would help before he resorted to other ways of attempting to clear his head.

He took his time walking through his family's home, stopping to look at photos on the wall along the way. He noticed there was one of him and Derika's post-wedding event and everyone including Lavinia was smiling. He checked on the children then he gently knocked on the door to the bedroom he and Derika shared, which his mother referred to as the second master suite. Growing up, he and Josiah wondered why the house was so big when there were only four of them. Lavinia told them because it was meant to be the family estate they could bring their children to one day.

Judah knocked on the door again and got no response. He figured Derika was mad but wanted to make sure before he made his bed in the office again. He opened the door and peered in. He saw Derika talking on the phone while typing away on her laptop.

"I'm sorry you feel that way Pat, but my husband has made a decision," he heard her say. "All I am asking is for you to give him three to six months… I hear you and I understand you, I do... He's perfectly capable but what he is doing right now is not about money, it's about legacy. I give you my word, I'll call you and only you as soon as Judah is ready… I appreciate you… I'll discuss that when I see you in LA… Thank you."

"Hey," Judah made his presence known to her. "I knocked but I don't think you heard me."

"Lock the door," she told him. "If you and I are going to get in a conversation, I will not have your mother barging in here assuming I'm being a contentious wife. Where were you?"

"I was doing some work in Daddy's office," he locked the door while trying to read her mood.

"I'm sorry I haven't been by the hospital these past few days," she said. "I've been busy trying to keep Judah 3:16 in people's good graces. Working on Pacific time. They are going to keep touring featuring other artists covering your leads. Ruby will also be getting a pay raise and I'm creating a title for her."

"Thank you for that," he said. "I appreciate you being on top of things. The band told me you took care of them."

"I take care of everybody," Derika said, getting up and putting her things in the chair. "I took care of JJ after he fell off his bike yesterday. I took care of Ms. Ann when she needed to leave early. I took care of Shay when she thought the keyboard player was her true love."

"What?" Judah raised an eye.

"Nothing happened," she promised him. "He actually told her no fraternizing within the band and that you threatened all of them."

"Good," Judah nodded, sensing she was in a good mood.

"And I take care of you even when you make me so mad I could kick you," she put her arms around him.

"I'm sorry, Dee," Judah rubbed her shoulders. "I can't do this alone."

"Then why did you leave me out of such a big decision?" she asked. "We don't do that. I feel like if you're going to do that, then what is the point of what we have."

"I just sat there and they decided," he told her. "It happened so fast."

"As your mother intended," Derika sighed. "I will not compete with her."

"Babe, I'm not asking you to," Judah said. "I admit, this was something we should have discussed together but you know I need you. Please?"

Derika didn't say anything.

"Or I have to sleep in the office again?" he asked. "That sofa is a bit uncomfortable."

"I didn't tell you take your ass on the sofa in the first place," she said. "You chose to go down there instead of deal with things from the jump."

"Well, I'm up here now," he said. "And I am sorry."

She looked into his eyes. He knew what she was looking for.

"I told you I'm not doing anything," he promised her. "I can't now, especially with church."

"Maya told you about this," she said, running a hand over his beard. "You do need to shave."

"I'll do it later," he told her.

Derika reached into the pocket in her robe and pulled out a blindfold.

"What are you doing?" he asked her as she put it over his eyes.

"You need me," Derika said as she welcomed him back into their bed. "And I need you. So before all this stuff gets out of control can we please just try?"

"What are you doing?" he asked, feeling her loosening his belt. "I'm just glad we're good again. You don't have to do that."

"Stop talking and keep on the blindfold," she advised, undressing him. "How long have we been here now? And I just realized it's no wonder we're both on edge. We have made time for everything else but this."

"Derika... you know I don't like doing anything in my parents' house," Judah objected, pushing her back.

"Touch me again and I swear I'll cuff you," she slapped him.

"So it's like that, huh?" he asked, touching his jaw. "Code word?"

"You figure it out," she whispered, unbuttoning his shirt and running her fingernails across his chest.

Judah exhaled quietly, feeling her lips on his stomach. She was right. Since they had been in Atlanta, it was one thing after the other and an emotional roller coaster. He allowed the thoughts that had been clouding his mind to float away as he felt his body crave her. He didn't realize just how stressed he had been lately until she began relieving him, taking him deeper down her throat, causing him to moan loudly. Her lips and tongue knew every nerve to hit with him and she knew exactly when to stop to leave him on edge. As she stroked his shaft with her hand, he felt her tease his balls for a moment and then go even further, rimming him and stimulating him more.

"You going to need to stop that, Dee," he panted, taking the blindfold off.

"I told you to keep that on," Derika stopped and let her hair fall.

"Where the hell you been?" he noticed the collection of items she had for them.

"Getting some stress relievers," she shrugged.

"Turn around," he instructed her. "Take that off and get on your knees."

She complied, arching her back, eager to be dominated. It was as if she felt a surge of electricity down her spine and in her thighs as he penetrated her. She tried catching her breath as the intensity increased and knew she couldn't hold off much longer. He felt her release and switched up on her, not yet at his climax.

"Hold up," she panted. "Wait…"

"What is it?" he asked.

"I want to try some of this stuff," she reached for some of the toys. "Which one shall we play with first?"

"Dee… we really don't need anything," he told her.

"Put this on," she handed him the hollow.

"Baby I really don't need to," he said.

"Fine," she said, putting it to her lips before inserting it between her legs. "Then I'll use it myself. And I want to see what happens when we have the stimulating cream."

This was the part of Derika that Lavinia feared. She worked hard to keep her sons from Delilahs who used their sexual prowess to make them lose their strength and common sense. Judah knew Derika knew his weaknesses and their intimate moments were an Achilles heel to him.

"Codeword is home," she said, putting a collar on his neck.

"Derika we really shouldn't in here," he said.

"Who the fuck is Derika?" she tightened the collar.

"Nothing," he said.

"Nothing?" she tightened it again. "Nothing who?"

"Nothing mistress," he said.

"Better," she smiled. "I can see where I have to teach you some manners. Clean my cunt juice off of this with your tongue."

Judah looked at the hollow she had just used on herself as she held it right to his mouth. This is where he truly enjoyed her dominance, as she would do things to make him feel vulnerable and submissive. He did as she instructed and broke for a moment as he leaned over to kiss her knowing that the moment was far from over and that they both needed to reach that place with each other they hadn't been in some time.

CHAPTER 7

"Good morning," Lavina greeted Judah and Derika when they entered the kitchen the following morning. "You two know how I keep my home. It's almost ten and y'all just strolling in. The children are already up and out and you missed the predawn morning prayer line with ministers, Interim-Bishop Waters. You have the title now please fulfill the role."

"I'm easing into the role," Judah said sitting at the table.

"Pardon me for thinking effective immediately had a different meaning," Lavinia shrugged. "The trays are still out so please get something to eat so that the staff can clean. We run a schedule in this house. And please, you are not a teenager. You know I hate seeing you look like that. Dress how you want to be addressed."

"Mama I'm home," he shook his head. "I get to be casual at home please."

"You answering me back?" Lavinia asked him.

"You look beautiful this morning Lavinia," Derika said as she loudly put a cover on a tray. "Would you mind sharing your hair stylist's number?"

"She only works with human hair, not synthetic, and she owns her own line," Lavinia said. "But yes, for Sunday, I'll be sure to connect you because you could use it."

"That's very kind of you Mama," Judah said.

"Girl, what are you doing?" Lavinia asked Derika as she sat next to Judah and began to eat. "Fix his plate first. It's disrespectful to feed yourself or others before the king of your house is fed first. Who raised you?"

"I can get my own eggs and sausage and grits," Judah said. "We are equal partners."

"Rachel knew better," Lavinia sipped her tea. "God designed the man to lead not go half on a household. There are standards. Nearly ten years in and you don't know how to take care of a husband? Judah, raise your voice and step up in your home. Then again when you ain't used to eating properly seasoned food like I cooked for you and your brother it's no wonder you have to go in the kitchen yourself."

"I can cook," Derika rolled her eyes.

"Then why is my son so skinny?" asked Lavinia.

"Mama, you know Daddy's side of the family is tall and slim," Judah reminded her.

"Your father was fattened up by the time we got married and I got the ring because of my ham and peach cobbler," Lavinia beamed. "A real wife knows how to fatten her family. I don't know what kind of diet she got y'all on out there in California. Last time the children ate properly from her it's when she was breastfeeding."

Derika slammed down her fork and turned to Lavinia.

"I am looking forward to service on Sunday!" Judah spoke up before Derika had the chance to respond. "You know Mama, I appreciate you allowing us to stay in the big bedroom upstairs especially since JJ is in my room. And you did a beautiful job with Maya's room. Dee was just saying how cute it is. "

"Yes," Derika added after feeling Judah's hand on her leg. "I thought we should stay elsewhere but it's nice to have the children experience a bit of their father's childhood. I was so happy to see you let Maya put some touches in there."

"This house is used to little boys, not a prissy, sassy little girl," Lavinia said. "It's nice to have someone appreciate my lace and ask to try on my hats and gloves and admire me. She will be taking etiquette classes while here though. Thank me later."

"How thoughtful of you," Derika said.

Judah gave Derika a smile of approval and got up to fix his plate and get some coffee. Lavinia glanced at Derika then shook her head when she heard Judah singing to himself.

"Well, if you are going to be living here for a while, I don't have a problem giving you tips to make this transition easier for all of us," Lavina said as she played with the pearl on her necklace. "In turn, I would appreciate you respecting these walls are rather thin, the halls echo and there are some things a mother does not need to hear her child doing or saying until three o'clock in the morning. Said 'oh God!' so many times I didn't know if y'all were praying or playing. If y'all going to be doing all that, warn me to leave or at least cover up the vent."

Derika couldn't even glance at Judah due to embarrassment. He sat down and ate as if nothing was out of the ordinary.

"Of course, I want grandchildren but I don't need to hear them being made!" Lavinia continued. "Judah, you know I sleep light and do checks at night especially with your father not home. My midnight prayer session was interrupted and you owe me and God an apology. Interesting how you ran away from being spanked back then but you can request it now. Spare the rod, boy."

"Oh my gosh!" Derika covered her face.

"I should hope the children are not exposed to hearing that lewd banter," Lavinia continued. "Then again they do sleep through everything including Sunday service. Don't know how to act because y'all take them to concerts but not to church out there in California. At least you are married but for all that is holy keep it down. What you need to do is turn it off. Both of you need to be on a fast, including a fast from the flesh."

"You do realize that's the first time since all of this stuff happened that we -" Judah began.

"No sir," Lavinia stopped him. "Your father dealt with you boys in that department and I want no parts of it. I'm not getting into your marital business. You know I do not overstep into your affairs."

"We will do our best to keep it down," Judah smiled as he put an arm around Derika. "Besides, you always said marriage was an honorable thing. I can soundproof the room if you want me to."

"Boy, loose her!" Lavinia clapped her hands once and scolded him. "After all what I heard last night I'm surprised the both of you are still standing. Just disgraceful. And if I find any marks on my wall, my headboard, or my son, Delilah -"

"Derika, Mama," Judah sighed.

"I said what I said and she acknowledged it," Lavinia said. "This is a holy house. And you, you were raised here. You ought to be ashamed. Don't make me have to separate you."

"I'm grown," Judah laughed, getting up to get juice from the counter.

"I said what I said," she repeated.

"I heard you," Judah leaned to kiss Lavinia's cheek.

"No thank you!" Lavinia pulled back. "I don't know what you've done with your mouth."

Derika wished the floor could just swallow her whole. She welcomed any interruption and was relieved when there was one.

"Good morning!" Paul greeted them as he walked into the dining room.

"Pastor Jones, it's always a good morning when you're around," Lavinia smiled. "Please join us for a late breakfast. I was just about to go over some duties, rules and regulations with these two. Do you have the guides?"

"I do," Paul said, holding up some books.

"I need you to go through these books about your roles in the church," Lavinia said to Judah and Derika. "I expect this to be a very easy transition as you two have had exposure to Greater Gates. Judah, please watch some of your brother and father's sermons. That's the preferred style of ministering. Derika, I especially need you to go over your duties in depth. You can not and will not make a mockery of me, this house or this ministry. By the way Judah, no denim, no graphic tees, no tattoos showing and no sweatpants. And them tight pants are a hell to the no. All that Judah 3:16 style is not meant for the sanctuary. Now Derika, what have you decided to wear? This is your debut and I expect a standard."

"Alphonso is making this beautiful red gown -" Derika began.

"No he's not," Lavinia interrupted her abruptly. "Red is for harlots, white is for wives. But as we are still in mourning, gray or navy blue is what you're wearing."

"I like to see her in red," Judah said, rubbing Derika's back. "I told Alphonso whatever color she wants. Besides, I pick out a lot of her clothes."

"Then when she's home you can pick out all the red you want for her," Lavinia shrugged. "During an ordination at Greater Gates, she will wear what she is told. And it better be tea-length. Now for the children, I was thinking Maya can wear something yellow, but certainly not Easter style, and I'll take care of her hair. Give it a little blowout at the Dominicans. She would look so lovely in that with pearls and a little bow."

"I'm not straightening her hair yet," Derika said.

"Dear, you ought to focus on your own hair," Lavinia replied. "I will call my stylist up and see if she has time for an install because God will not say I did not do my duty. Judah, trim your beard a bit. Do not shave it. You look too young shaved and we need an older, trustworthy face right now."

Derika looked at Judah and wondered if it was worth it. She agreed to three months but knew he was going to stay as long as he was needed. She hated the protocol and fakeness of people she met in church. She also hated the fact that she had millions on the line with their projects delayed.

"I signed up for Judah Waters not Greater Gates and not Lavinia," Derika whispered to him as Lavinia and Paul chatted. "This is important to you so I'll try but you keep your mother away from me."

"That's all I ask," Judah kissed her head.

"See… and all this public kissing needs to stop," Lavinia told them. "This is too much cuddling. Have some respect that some of us are getting nausea from just watching you. Derika stop letting him do that, you hear me? No self-respecting woman lets a man do that in public."

"I think it's sweet," Paul chimed in. "Marriage is a beautiful thing to see on a young couple."

"If it was so sweet you'd be married," Lavinia told him.

"First Lady?" one of the maids poked her head in. "There's a woman from the art gallery?"

"Oh yes," Lavinia said, getting up. "I'll be just a minute."

"Try harder," Judah encouraged Derika as soon as Lavinia was out of earshot.

"Judah, I have had enough of her," Derika looked at him. "I can't do this if she keeps at it. I can't even look at her after what she said. Judah either you get us our own place or keep her away from me."

Judah and Paul exchanged glances knowing both women had strong personalities and neither was going to back down.

"May I suggest you meet with Fiona Prescott, Derika?" Paul offered. "She's taken over duties from Rachel in the women's ministries. She's needing some help and I am sure you two will hit it off just fine."

"I don't want to be a part of the women's ministry," Derika told him.

"But with Judah as Interim-Bishop, you must as it's tradition," he told her. "Bishop's wife always heads it."

"Suppose you had a bishop who is unmarried or a widow?" Derika asked.

"Derika is more behind the scenes," Judah explained. "She isn't even the type to sit on the stage during service. And I know she's not going to be into the whole bringing remarks thing."

"You two have so much stacked against you," Paul shook his head. "Your father and brother were in the middle of using their own money to save the church from folding. We have a few people wanting to more or less buy it out to merge congregations. Lavinia put your name down because you are the only adult male family member who can sit at the helm. It's not because she believes you can do it but because she needs your face there to keep them at bay. She knows you can bring a crowd. I believe your father will wake up and say what he wants done. But I also believe with the right help, you can do this. Both of you. So what do I need to know to help you overcome what is before you?"

"Well…" Derika said not knowing what to think.

"If I may Judah, er, Bishop," Paul handed him a paper. "I took the liberty of coming up with some suggestions for your sermon. It can flow a lot better if you break the ice by joining in on the end of praise and worship. By you already singing, I think that will eliminate Derika from having to be put on the spot of introducing you. And maybe Derika, don't wear a fancy hat but one of those little things they stick on."

"A fascinator?" she asked.

"I wouldn't know," Paul chuckled. "Come in as you are for the most part but enough to impress the elders but make the congregation see you as a positive. For instance Bishop, you can wear black denim pants with your collar and jacket."

Derika and Judah looked at each other and realized that Paul was truly valuable and understanding.

"Thank you, Pastor," Derika took the paper and looked over it.

"I know how close you and your brother were," Paul said to Judah. "He shared quite a few ideas with me and when you are ready, I would like to relay the ideas to you."

"I would like that very much," Judah extended a hand.

Derika watched them shake hands. For a brief moment, she wanted to pull Judah aside and tell him to just leave and return to their life. But she knew if it meant fulfilling Josiah's legacy, he would commit.

CHAPTER 8

Sunday came too fast for them. Judah and Derika looked at the closed doors leading to the main part of the church and listened as the service was going on. They had to walk down the aisle together as a family then Judah would take his place at the pulpit.

"The bass player is off," Judah spoke up. "String needs to be tuned. You hear it? And someone is in the soprano section who should be in the alto section. You heard it right there?"

"No," Derika looked down.

"Dee, we got this," he leaned to whisper in her ear. "By the way, you look fly as -"

She looked at him shocked he was about to drop an f-bomb. He burst out laughing and made her laugh as well.

"You thought I was going to say it huh?" he asked.

"I'm going to have to get used to… this," Derika said, looking at him in all black except for his collar. "You look… respectable. But I prefer the old kicks and colors."

"They are ready for you, Bishop," a deacon told them, handing Judah a wireless mic. "Just turn it on when you're ready."

"I'll signal you when it's time to wrap it up… Bishop," she smiled, putting an arm around JJ as Maya held Judah's hand.

"We are in this together," Judah put his other hand around Derika's waist.

Judah nodded to signal he was ready and then they walked in, all eyes on them. JJ and Maya were not phased by it, having seen such processions already. Lavinia had told them it was an honor and promised them treats after service so they were going to behave if only to get praise from their grandmother.

"Brothers and sisters, Interim-Bishop Judah Waters and First Lady Derika Waters," the moderator called as the musicians began playing one of Judah's songs.

Alphonso smiled when he saw Derika on the screen wearing a beautiful black gown with large red accents. Lavinia looked down from her seat on the stage, next to her husband and son's empty chairs and lowered her head so her hat could cover how her eyebrows were arched in an angry expression brought on by seeing how Derika defied her by wearing a fitted dress. Lavinia made a note to remind the members that she would remain First Lady Waters, a title she enjoyed sharing with Rachel but would not let anyone refer to Derika as such.

Judah walked his family to the second row from the front, puzzling members for a moment as they wondered why the wife of the minister giving the sermon was not seated on stage.

"Greater Gates... isn't it a beautiful day to be in the house of the Lord?" Judah turned on the mic as the church attendees responded excitedly with cheers and shouts. "Before I get into the word, do you mind if I join the choir right quick? I just want to go where the spirit is leading and acknowledge the true authority in this place. I also want to take a moment to acknowledge the woman who is the reason why I am here, who covered me in prayer and encouraged me to show up and let God have his way."

Lavinia stood up and smiled.

"Derika, thank you," Judah looked down at his wife. "A lot of people have no idea what you do behind the scenes and I appreciate everything you do for our family. I just wanted to say that because I don't say it enough. I know it's tradition for the wife to introduce the incoming but my wife prefers to not distract from the message and I find that so humbling of her. Bro. Alphonso, y'all ready?"

"We're ready Bishop!" Alphonso nodded.

As Lavinia sat, ready to give Judah a piece of her mind for not acknowledging her, Derika and Paul exchanged quick glances with each other, agreeing that Judah had already won the congregation's trust.

Lavinia was proud of Judah as he took time to learn as much as he could and listen to church concerns. She was far less impressed that he wore regular clothes through the week, not a suit like his brother. Derika stayed out of Lavinia's way and only went by the church if Judah needed her to step in to give her opinion on something quickly. Derika also missed the looks she was getting from various women in the church as weeks went by.

"Derika?" Fiona had stopped Derika after service a few Sundays later. "Is everything okay?"

"Yes, of course," Derika smiled. "Why?"

"It's just that we had a luncheon the other day and gave a tribute to Rachel," Fiona told her. "We had hoped you would've been there. Luckily, First Lady Waters happened to pass by and said a few words. I know your work comes first but you also have duties to attend to with us. And I don't think it's fair you are so distant with us. Rachel spoke so highly of you and even said how she wanted you to be one of the speakers at our annual women's conference. You've never given us a chance to get to know you and I am starting to believe First Lady when she said that you have no intention of connecting with us or supporting Greater Gates. This is like the eighth invitation you rejected and you're never in your office."

Derika knew exactly what was going on without having to ask Fiona for more information.

"Do you have my cellphone number?" Derika asked. "Text me next time. Do not go through my secretary or Lavinia."

"At this point, I'm just not sure I want to," Fiona sighed.

"I've had a lot to juggle lately," Derika told her. "Are you and Deacon Nick joining us at the house for dinner? Or is it lunch? I'm not used to it just yet but maybe we can take a moment and catch up?"

"Oh, no I didn't get an invitation," Fiona said.

"That Judah," Derika sighed. "He must have forgotten. Please, we had you on this list and wanted you to bring the children since they are close in age to ours. Maya and JJ could use some friends."

"Thank you," Fiona said. "I'll let Nick know."

"Good save, Dee," Derika said quietly as she got into her vehicle.

"Mommy…" she heard Maya chirp. "I'm not buckled."

"JJ please buckle your sister," Derika told her son.

"I'm busy," he said looking at his phone.

"Maya, buckle yourself up," Derika said.

"I can't!" Maya whined.

"Hey Dee!" Derika's front door opened. "Can you drop me by Jason?"

"Shay, don't be sneaking up on me like that," Derika warned. "Buckle up Maya for me. And who the hell is Jason?"

"He comes to the morning service but he works at a restaurant," Shay told her as she got in the front and turned around to help Maya.

"Does this Jason know you?" Derika asked.

"Of course he does," Shay told her.

"Does he know you, know you like in the biblical sense?" Derika looked at her.

"Of course not!" Shay told her. "I'm a lady."

"And you're going to stay a lady, that's why I'm dropping you home," Derika told her. "Home to your house or you can come to the Waters' house for this dinner. And why is it Sunday dinner if it's in the afternoon?"

"If I come by you, you paying me to babysit?" Shay asked.

"Yes," Derika told her.

"As you should," Shay smiled.

"Give me the tea on Fiona Prescott and Rachel's little group," Derika told her. "I need to be up to date before I get home."

"You trying to be a real first lady huh?" Shay asked.

"You know I am not into this shit," Derika said.

"Mommy you're going to hell!" Maya gasped. "That's a bad word!"

"Maya put on your headphones," Shay said, giving them to her before turning back to Derika. "Okay. So let's have a crash course on the Greater Gates women."

Derika tried taking in as much as she could from Shay before they got to the house. Shay went off with the children while Derika joined the adults in the parlor then in the dining room. Derika sat quietly and watched how Judah seamlessly flowed in the conversation with the visiting ministers. They sat at the mahogany table Lavinia had spent a fortune on which could comfortably seat about twenty-four. Derika was not a person who liked to be touched and yet everyone expected a hug and a wise word from her. She hated being asked about the women's events and children's events as if that was all women were designed for but was happy Shay had put her up to speed on things.

"How are you adjusting to the role of First Lady?" one of the ladies asked Derika.

"Now my husband isn't dead yet!" Lavinia inserted herself. "As the senior and more active, we've decided First Lady is how I shall be referred to while Derika is fine with Mrs. Waters or her name. Win win don't you think?"

"Well if given the opportunity to serve instead of having my calls intercepted I would absolutely love to oversee and ensure that the groundwork my sister-in-law put in is carried out to fruition," Derika spoke up. "The adjustment is not easy because I never thought I'd be doing something like this. My husband and his brother were always talking on the phone or connecting with each other, so that gave Rachel and I the opportunity to share so much of our dreams and visions and personal lives with each other. She had some wonderful ideas and what I loved about her and Josiah was that they wouldn't have an idea for one day, they would have an idea that would extend ten or twenty years into the future. I definitely cannot fill her shoes but I absolutely would love to ensure that what she started is carried through to completion. The shelter is the main project. So many men and teen boys are not allowed in shelters with their mother. Raising funds for that project is paramount and Sis. Fiona Prescott here is working harder than anyone to secure the right location. She is also continuing the women's conference which is our biggest draw at the church. She and Rachel earned over eleven thousand dollars considering the past three years. I've already spoken to a few of our actress and singer friends to attend the next event and I am very excited to see where she takes it. Rachel trusted her and so do I. I'm not trying to break tradition but I'm absolutely all for Fiona continuing as she has and would happily nominate her to a formal position."

"It's an honor to serve," Fiona smiled as Nick held her hand.

Fiona was taken aback by Derika's knowledge of her work. The other women exchanged smiles of approval while Lavinia quickly drank her iced tea.

"I think a lot of people are forgetting that Judah agreed to do this on an interim basis and I am certain whoever replaces him will do an excellent job based on the plans Josiah laid," Derika concluded. "Jo... Bishop Josiah, he was excellent and chosen for this. I'm just glad he was able to share the vision so Judah could stand in temporarily."

"How blessed you are to have her," one of the women remarked to Lavina as Derika received approving looks, including a nod from Fiona.

"I'm sure this is nothing like traveling the world or your celebrity lifestyle," a deacon noted. "Is this something you can handle?"

"It's different," Derika smiled politely. "I'm accustomed to being by my husband's side when it comes to business and co-parenting and marriage, but when it comes to the church, definitely it is an adjustment because not only does he take the lead but it's such a huge lead that there is no point in me offering to assist. And outside of my grandmother taking me to church whenever I visited her for a few weeks, I really don't have much of a church background. My parents were far more spiritual than they were religious and they were not fans of the business of church. My parents had gone through it. Where they needed a lot of help from the church, they were hurt. They went from being a young couple in need to being a young couple who were confident that they would never want their child to experience hurt. My grandmother was one of those people who gave her last into charity and church and at the end of the day she died almost penniless. In fact, if it were not for Judah intervening we would have had to pay the church my grandmother loved so much to eulogize her."

"Simple misunderstanding," Lavinia smiled. "Excuse me while I check on dessert."

"I'm just amazed Bishop Judah hid you from us for so long," someone chuckled. "This is my first time officially meeting you Lady Derika and I'm most impressed. I don't blame you though Bishop for keeping her to yourself. She's lovely and I'd hide her too."

Derika excused herself to check on the children when she got a text message from Shay that they were in the kitchen.

"Oh, your dress!" Derika sighed looking at the mess Maya made when she saw them. "Did Shay see this?"

"I wanted to get us cupcakes but the tray fell down," Maya said as the other children watched. "It tastes good. You want some?"

"I'm sorry Ms. Derika," one of the maids apologized. "Shay went to use the bathroom but two seconds ago and this accident just happened. I'm sorry."

"It's not your fault so please don't apologize," Derika told her while wiping the dress.

"Of course it isn't," Lavinia said, slicing her cake. "Any mother with common sense would've changed her out of the dress if she is too young to feed herself and tell her to ask, not take. Then you bring Marco Sanchez's daughter here without permission. I don't know why Judah takes to that girl so much. You know, her father got killed in a drug deal gone bad. After all that time Judah thought I didn't know he used to bail him out or pay cops to turn the other way. He ran over Judah just like you're letting his daughter run over you. Taking in strays. God helps those who help themselves. You don't even know how to control your own children. Thank God they are here with me."

"JJ why don't you and Maya wait for Shay with your new friends upstairs?" Derika suggested, prompting the children to run off.

Derika got up and walked up to Lavinia. The ladies in the kitchen watched silently expecting a confrontation.

"You want to talk about my mothering skills, old woman?" asked Derika. "There are things I am dealing with now with my husband because of the half-assed mothering bullshit you did years ago. And leave Marco's name out your mouth because we both know what really happened that night. Do not come for that girl. She was a child and barely remembers him. I am so sick and tired of you and I can not wait to go back home and get Judah back on track."

"If you don't get thee behind me Satan I will send you on a one-way ticket to the pit of hell," Lavinia pointed the knife at Derika. "Are you crazy? Don't you ever come this close to me while I'm holding a knife! The good book says if it offends thee, cut it off. And the rate you been going, somebody might finely chop you up."

"I wish you would," Derika stepped closer.

"Miss Lavinia, I can finish this for you," Anna took the knife from her hand. "Maybe you can see if your guests are allergic to nuts or dairy?"

"Delilah ain't woman enough," Lavinia told Anna.

"Derika!" Derika told her slamming a hand on the counter. "As in Mrs. Derika Waters as in your son gave me the name. But since you want to come up on me, why did you order my secretary to send everything to you?"

"You seemed busy in your career," Lavinia shrugged but spoke in a gentler tone. "I was trying to help you. Look, I love my son too. You focus on his career, let me focus on the church. You trying to do my job and you won't have a job for yourself. Maybe you ought to go home for a week or two and see people face to face to ensure Judah has his affairs in order."

Derika folded her arms and looked down. She wasn't accustomed to Lavinia being nice.

"Your cheesecake is really delicious, by the way," she mumbled. "Judah wants me to get the recipe."

"Maya is learning my recipes," Lavinia told her. "But if that's your way of agreeing with me, then say it. Like I said, we both want what is best for him. And to be honest, a woman needs to be in her house now and again. There is only one queen in this kingdom and it's me. Go to your own castle. I'll look after the children, and Judah will be fine. Make yourself useful and grab a tray. A lady always makes an entrance presenting a well-received recipe."

Derika watched Lavina as she walked out and looked back at Anna. "Do you think she would have?" Derika asked, looking at the knife. "When it comes to her boys, yes, she would have," Anna replied. "If I were you, I'd take out them desserts, and then fly out to California so y'all can get a break from each other. Y'all two been running up my blood pressure in here so I know Judah is frustrated. It might be a good thing. Don't worry, if you go, I will personally keep an eye on the children. For your sanity, go."

CHAPTER 9

Derika took Lavinia's advice to get away and invited Judah to join her for at least the first week. At the last minute, he decided to stay when doctors told him that his father could be transferred from the hospital to hospice. He insisted on Darold returning home and placed him in a downstairs guest room. He instructed house staff to fill the room with photos, scents and other things that would help him come back. He also advised them to leave the door open and not worry if the children were making too much noise as doctors said it was possible he might be able to hear things.

Judah suggested to Derika to take Shay along so she wouldn't get too lonely and at the same time, start preparing her for the side of the industry she was eventually going to see. He also insisted she let Pat Smith know they were still interested in his offer and she went straight from the airport to Pat's office.

"She's going to end up in the secular market," Pat told Derika during their meeting after observing Shay through a glass window. "Judah was right about her being the next big thing but there is no way I'm going to invest in a gospel career for her. She is perfect in looks with the hair and complexion and height. Great sound, great back story with a dad in trouble over drugs then eventually getting shot, but too soft to compete with these women who will drag her through social media. Her image has to adjust. Prepare her if you want to protect her. It's better she hears it from you than learn the hard way."

"That's it?" Derika asked.

"Is Shay her real name?" Pat asked.

"Xiomara," Derika told him.

"Now that ups the ante," Pat smiled. "Use that instead of Shay when it's time to launch. So how is she with reggaeton?"

"She barely speaks Spanish," Derika drank a bit more. "No bueno."

"Doesn't matter," Pat said. "I'll invest. She's a dimond needing to be shaped but I see a package there even if her voice isn't iconic."

Derika watched him watching Shay. She wasn't sure what he saw in her.

"Do I have to keep her from you?" Derika asked Pat.

"That's a brazen question," he seemed offended.

"But a valid one," she told him. "A barely legal afrolatina with a cute body and face in this market? I'm not putting her in the boat and watching sharks circle her. So again, Mr. Smith, do I have to protect her from you?"

"I like you Derika," Pat chuckled. "I like you a lot. You take your drinks like you ask your questions - straight. Do you think you have to protect her from me?"

"You have power and a penis," Derika told him. "Of course I do."

"I have children older than her," he told her. "I am a man who prefers women not girls. Girls are clingy, expensive and trouble. Women are different."

"I still don't trust you," Derika finished off her drink.

"That's on you," he said. "By the way, what's your size? There's an event at the mansion this evening. You can change there and I'll have my secretary arrange a stylist."

"No thank you," Derika said.

"Send the kid home and I'll see you later," Pat said. "Excuse me."

"Didn't you hear me?" Derika asked.

"I've already spoken to your husband and he said you would be attending," Pat told her. "Amazed he took my call since he's been so busy lately. Him playing church is costing me money. So you need to show up and prove it's still on. Let's call it a show of good faith. Now if you'll excuse me, I have a quick meeting to attend to. Do not keep me waiting."

Derika watched him walk in to say a few words to Shay and then leave. She felt her phone vibrate and saw a message from Judah wishing her well for that evening and told her that Ruby was able to take Shay for the weekend. Derika did not like when people went behind her back to speak to Judah directly after they confirmed something with her.

"Judah… you need to pick up this phone," Derika said when she called and was sent to voicemail. "You know I hate going to these things alone… Call me later. And kiss the children for me."

"You want me to come with you?" Ruby asked Derika when she picked up Shay.

"No," she replied. "Just keep an eye on her for me. I'll call you tomorrow. Pat will likely turn this into an all-nighter than ends with brunch."

"Lucky you!" Ruby smiled.

"Lucky me," Derika forced a smile wondering what Ruby would say if she really knew the depth of things.

Derika agreed when she got home that Pat was right that Shay needed to understand some harsh truths about the industry and be ready to compete with the other women. Shay spent her time playing in Judah's studio and swimming in the pool, Derika tried a few times to find the right moment to talk to her.

"You need to because that girl is greener than a field in springtime," Ruby agreed when Derika asked if she felt Shay needed an awakening. "She is far too innocent to be going on the road and I've already noticed people are waiting for the right moment to pounce."

"I'm not sure how to talk to her," Derika said.

"Stop seeing her as a little girl and see her as a client and as a mentee," Ruby shrugged. "Tell her what happened to you before it happens to her. And show her the real you she may not know."

Derika eventually took Shay to dinner and was halfway listening until she heard Shay gushing about a young man at church.

"He's just so handsome and sweet and I can already see us having a church together and a family," Shay smiled, talking about the latest boy who had piqued her interest. "He plays bass -"

"Jason?" Derika asked.

"Oh no, I'm over him," Shay said. "He's dating a girl at the restaurant. This is the bass player at Greater Gates. He just started college."

"Another musician, Shay?" Derika sighed, sipping her wine. "You know why me and Judah work out so well? Because he knows everything about music and instruments and I can't sing in tune for more than ten minutes or even play a triangle. I already told you to leave band members and musicians. Creatives are not easy people. Two creatives is a problem. A creative needs a logical person, a parent or a handler."

Derika put down her fork and called to the waiter as Shay played with her curls.

"Get me something fruity with a lot of gin or vodka in it and bring my goddaughter a tropical martini," Derika ordered. "And don't water down my shit either. I need it strong."

"Dee, we're Christian," Shay said as the waiter walked off. "We're not supposed to drink alcohol or use that language."

"Then why did Jesus get the party lit by turning water into wine?" Derika shrugged. "After hearing you talk all that 'I'm praying for a man' bullshit we both need a drink."

"I'm not even twenty-one," Shay said.

"Exactly," Derika pointed out. "You have so much life to live and yet you are here with your little image of a church wife in your head when you have yet to taste your first drink or leave the country or go to college or drive a car. I bet you haven't even fucked yet."

Shay looked embarrassed to hear Derika speak so candidly.

"Can you even say the word fuck?" Derika asked her. "You do know that men in ministry have expectations of their wives right? And once that door closes, there is no praise and worship. It's a lot of words that are said and a lot of things that you don't even know about that you're going to have to do. Has your mother even explained to you the power of a pussy?"

"I… I…" Shay took a sip of her drink the waiter brought her and gagged.

"If you think this tastes awful, imagine when liquor is the only thing you have to gargle with after a man cums in your mouth," Derika sipped her drink. "Waiter… you watered my shit down!"

"Dee, I'm sorry but I don't know who you are right now," Shay found her voice. "Are you tipsy?"

"You don't know me and you don't know Judah," Derika told her. "I am sorry I had to be that vivid with you but honestly, that's how a lot of people in our world speak when they are not on that stage. That's what a lot of people do behind closed doors. Baby, I love you, and I have to give you a reality check. You are not ready for this world. Judah isn't going to always be there and you need him and you need me if only to help you find someone trustworthy. You see he hasn't even been able to work with you or finish his own projects since this church thing. It's too much. I have a few people who want to work with you and they are not gospel. You can make a lot of money but I'm not sure you are ready."

Shay was dumbfounded but at the same time realized that Derika was right. She had been living in a dreamland and as her mind replayed things, she realized she had seen some things that were odd to her and wondered what they knew.

"You change a lot when you're here," Shay told her. "Like your clothes and makeup and the people you hang out with. You'd never wear that to church."

"First of all, my husband picked out this outfit," Derika said, fully aware of how low cut and tight-fitting her outfit was. "Second of all, why have I never seen you in a mini skirt or midriff top? We are going shopping this weekend to make you look like the age you are. And we will put it on your godfather's black card because we can."

"As we should!" Shay smiled.

Shay was interested in a makeover and always wanted to dress a little edgier. But with school uniforms her whole life, she just stuck to jeans and basic tops. She had always enjoyed watching Derika get dressed to go out and loved going into her closet. It was too good an offer to resist.

"Shay, you know I love you right?" Derika leaned in to get her attention.

"Of course I do," Shay replied. "It's just that we're taught one thing and then it's like not real and I've been praying so hard and now I don't know what to think."

"Your relationship with God is your own," Derika told her. "You have prayer but you also need common sense sweetheart. I think it's time to tell you my truth. You have a talent, a gift. But you are also a beautiful girl and a young girl. Men in this world smell virginity and naivety. The thing is people do judge women based on how they look in every industry and you are ripe for the grooming. How far you go depends on who owns you. Do you understand what I'm trying to say?"

"Yes ma'am," Shay nodded, squinting her face as she tried Derika's drink. "I think so. You want me to do more secular stuff, not gospel?"

"Drink a little more," Derika told her. "I am going to watch you learn to hold your liquor but I am also going to teach you to know if someone may have messed with your drink. I am going to watch you sample things with a sound mind rather than under pressure so you do not have to do things you don't want to. It's a gentle breaking in so to speak."

"So it's like training me so that I don't have to learn the hard way?" Shay asked.

"Pretty much," Derika nodded. "First of all, even Christians sin. They are just good at hiding it. This part is very important - don't you ever meet anybody behind closed doors, I don't care who they are or what they're trying to offer you. Don't you ever go to a meeting by yourself and don't ever be alone in the studio by yourself. Be very careful when it comes to getting a ride with somebody or accepting the opportunity to go with them for a private session. You're young and you're beautiful but you're gullible and you want it so bad and you want to please everybody and unfortunately they will prey on you and use you and pass you around until… until the only way to get rid of it is to fill yourself with poison and try to block all of what's happening."

"I promise you I am smarter than I look," Shay told her. "People keep thinking I can't handle life but I can. I got my shit in order. I'm smart."

Derika took a deep breath and stared at her drink for a moment.

"Back in the day, I thought I was smart too but I wasn't music industry or entertainment industry smart," said Derika. "I was street smart and book smart. I haven't shared this story with a lot of people but I'm going to share it with you. Back in those days Judah and I were not perfect and he did some things that are a part of his story to tell, not mine. I allowed myself to get caught up and started getting a lot of attention from a lot of people and between me doing my thing and Judah doing his, we had a bunch of mixers we attended night after night. We were close friends but we were dating other people. The one rule we had was to check in with each other every few minutes. I had a couple of pills, a couple of shots, light stuff compared to the heroin and cocaine that was available."

"Was he into that heavy stuff?" Shay asked. "I asked because I saw something in his shaving kit before. I never told anyone that I saw, I promise. But he said he was delivered from addiction but does he still do it?"

"Yeah," Derika nodded. "When he was younger, he had to go to rehab. The label threatened to drop him if it got out. I made sure he didn't slip up or at least have too much. Use and abuse are two different things. But that's his story to tell. My story… That night I was telling you about… all I know is I had a drink and I woke up with somebody on top of me. I don't know if I screamed or was too scared to scream. The thing about it is I'm not even sure who it was and I believe it was more than one person. I blacked out again and it was over and I was there naked and sore and… I just put on my clothes and left. I was wearing black so the blood didn't show. I just went in the shower and cried."

"Are you sure you don't know who it was?" Shay's voice cracked. "No one saw on the cameras?"

"Even if the camera got it, it doesn't matter with powerful people," Derika quickly wiped a tear away. "What I do know is that I was saving myself for when I got married. I was robbed of it. It occurred during a tour. In my mind, I thought everybody was a Christian and saved and good and thinking of who was in that room, it was mostly gospel people so don't mind titles. Judah figured it out after a couple of weeks of me just seeming different to him and he blamed himself for not protecting me and for not realizing immediately. People thought we were dating but were just friends then. Even Darold was convinced we were a couple back then because Judah didn't want them in his personal affairs. But after that incident, he stepped up. The thing is when *he* told people we were together and they saw the ring, they automatically had respect for me because they had respect for him. You wouldn't have known any of this because you were a little girl when we got married."

"Dee... I am so sorry," Shay got up and hugged her.

Derika hugged her back.

"You don't have to be sorry," Derika smiled. "The thing is so many of us feel ruined when we have that taken away. Trauma takes time to overcome. Judah helped me overcome that."

"Thank you," Shay said. "For allowing me into your space and the circle and for wanting to be there as a mentor and friend."

"I thought I was family?" Derika gasped. "Mentor and friend?"

"You're like a mom to me, Dee," Shay hugged her again. "So Mama Dee? Auntie Dee? It don't matter. And if you want me to, I can tell you how to deal with those church cliques. It's not hard."

Derika accepted Shay's offer.

"Now I have another question for you," Derika said as Shay sat down and sipped some more of her drink. "Do you know what to look for before you put your mouth on a penis? Some STDs are tricky."

They looked at each other and burst into giggles. Shay realized she had entered Judah and Derika's closest circle and how valuable it was to have them in her life.

CHAPTER 10

A few nights later, Shay opened the door at the house after hearing the doorbell ring. She squealed when she saw who was on the other side.

"OMG you're Cameron Diggs!" she gushed upon seeing the star basketball player. "Can I?"

"No problem," he said, letting her take a selfie.

"My brother is going to die!" she swooned. "Well not really but. Are you coming to Atlanta for real?"

"Hey hey," Derika walked over after hearing the commotion. "Fangirl, down."

"Cam Diggs is at your house!" Shay said excitedly.

"I see that," Derika waved a hand to welcome him in. "I see you've met our goddaughter Shay."

Cameron had a presence about him that made him feel like a homeboy. He was tall, young and smooth-faced with friendly eyes and a distinctive charm.

"So what brings you to LA Shay?" Cameron asked.

"I was on the last tour," Shay tried composing herself. "I sing and my godfather is producing my album. Well, he was going to. I mean we did the duet but my single isn't released yet. But I'm thinking of doing a pop album first."

Derika smiled as she noticed Shay, in her new girly wardrobe, suddenly had enough confidence to talk to a top twenty draft pick.

"Church has y'all too busy to put out music?" Cameron asked. "Well, that's insane."

"It is hectic," Derika said. "Shay just made us some smoothies. Would you like one?

"Sure," he said, following them into the kitchen.

"So what brings you by unannounced?" Derika asked.

"I want you on my team, Mrs. Waters," Cameron told her. "You make things happen. People listen to you. Managers are managed by you. I spoke to your girl Thia at The Ambassador Agency and she said she got the PR if you got the management so manage."

"You drove all the way here for that?" she laughed. "I'm so sorry you wasted your time, Cameron. I would love to be on your team but right now, Judah is my priority and I know the music industry, not sports. Besides, I'm trying to get some stuff together for Shay."

"You know how to review contracts, identify a legit agent and recommend a good brand to align with," he said, taking a smoothie from Shay. "You know how to vet a publicist and select a stylist and shit, I bet you even know who to go to for interiors and catering. I want you on my team."

"Cameron, you are top tier which means whoever is managing you can't have anyone else on their roster," Derika shook her head. "It's the same with Judah."

"He's your husband but I'm a client and I can pay you double," he said. "By the way kid, this is some good stuff."

Shay giggled and twirled her hair around her finger.

"Shay, why don't you go downstairs and go over those bars for the audition," Derika suggested. "I'll be down there as soon as we wrap up."

"Okay," she nodded. "Nice meeting you Mr. Diggs."

"You can call me Cam," he smiled as she walked off. "Y'all going to have to keep an eye on that one."

"Don't worry, I'll go into lioness mode for her," Derika said as soon as she heard a door shut in the distance. "I thought I told you to please be respectful of my home and not show up as you want. I already told you I am not working with you."

"Well I want to work with you," he said leaning closer to her.

"I am a married woman," she reminded him. "You need to leave my husband's house."

"My bad," he laughed. "I'll be in Atlanta soon. Can we meet there?"

"Yes, we can but that doesn't change my mind when it comes to working with you," Derika said. "Please, let me show you to the door."

"You're going to manage me, Derika," Cameron told her as he walked out the door.

"I'll pray for you," Derika waved. "Bye now."

The rest of the trip went on without much drama and Derika was grateful to get back into business mode. She also realized how well she and Ruby worked together and working with Shay, they saw how important it was to prepare young artists for the real world.

"How are things with you and Judah?" Ruby asked Derika as they worked in silence in her office. "I catch service on the livestream now and again. He is really engaging as a speaker. I'm sure you are proud of him. "

"I can't wait for the day he quits," Derika confessed. "I am so tired of the routine, the church and don't get me started on his mother. You've met her. You think anyone will notice if she had an accident at the house one day?"

"Derika it's not that bad," Ruby laughed.

"It's worse," Derika sighed. "I really thought about leaving him for a while between church business and that bitch. I used to have his brother and father stand up for me and Rachel always had a kind word but Judah just seems to let his mother say what she wants. It's almost like he is afraid of her and disrespects me. I tell you one thing, after that knife incident, I will stab her ass if she tries anything."

"You wouldn't," Ruby shook her head. "You are too in love with him. And if you left him, it would go into a place so dark, I would hate to know what kind of self-harm he would end up doing. You two have carried so much for one person to ruin that. Do counseling. Do something. But you two need each other, if only because no one else in this world understands you. Moving on. I got another call from Cam Diggs today. Are you going to take him on if we form this agency or what?"

"Cameron is an athlete," Derika shrugged. "Athletes take a lot of time to manage and the publicists tend to be on call. I would like to stick to some safe clients in the industry we know first. If he calls again, tell him no."

"Are you sure?" Ruby asked. "He's determined to work with you. I guess you made an impression at the celebrity gospel basketball tournament. Got to admit, it was refreshing to see Judah can actually play a bit. We thought he was just tall for nothing."

"I guess that's what happens when you have a brother and a playmate in the same person growing up to practice with," Derika shrugged. "I'll speak to Cameron myself and let him know we will not be taking him."

"Dee, if you have him and Shay and I have the rest out here, we will be hitting two major cities at once," Ruby pointed out.

"It is Atlanta," Derika laughed. "I can stick to music and ministry. That place is the mecca for what we do. I am not bringing on some young athlete. And that is final."

CHAPTER 11

With Derika gone, Judah put more of an effort into studying his father's sermons and his brother's way of connecting to the congregation. He watched the videos of them while he sat with Darold barely listening to the caregiver Barbara updating him. He also sat in on several ministries to get better acquainted with them, but found himself drawn to sitting in the back of the sanctuary while listening to Alphonso pull out the best he could from the choir and praise team. The way their voices echoed throughout the empty room, the way the music just filled every crevice… it was magnetic.

"Sis. Johnson!" Alphonso called to a lead singer. "I need a soprano in an F out of your mouth, please! I need an F if only for the faith I need to get through tonight. All of y'all be doing too much."

"Alphonso, I'm trying," the woman replied. "We been here for two hours."

"Give the mic to Monica," Alphonso instructed her. "If it was Shay, she would try and stick it out for five hours. Young people are more excited. You don't want the honor of singing lead in my choir, then pass it along. That's why you are going to stay singing in that nightclub in East Point and never get to a downtown lounge. You know what… all of you… take ten, get some lemon and honey and water in them pipes. I need to pull out another song before you all ruin my service."

Judah chuckled as Alphonso passed him walking out of the main area. Alphonso hadn't noticed him sitting near the back pew.

"As if you could do better," Alphonso challenged him.

"Don't tempt me, old school," Judah warned him playfully.

"I might be old but I ain't cold," Alphonso told him, sitting down. "I got your old school. Don't act like I didn't know you before you became a bishop Mister 3:16. By the way, how's Mrs. Waters?"

"She's fine," Judah replied. "Being a better grandmother than she was a mother, I'll give her that."

"Why would I ask you about your mother when she's always here?" Alphonso shrugged. "How is your wife? Haven't seen her in service."

"She's good," Judah smiled. "Handling some business out west but doing great. Third time out there for the month."

"That's good she's occupied but I asked how she was in general," Alphonso cleared his throat. "Now Bishop, you know I mind my business, I really do, but the Lord has to use me sometimes and I say okay use me. We both know this church has a way of gossiping and the word on the street is that you are about to divorce?"

"Divorce?" Judah raised an eyebrow.

"All the single women are talking, honey," Alphonso said. "Especially them choir girls because you already know. They're single and desperate and ready for God to send them a Boaz to put a ring on it. I'm just saying, watch out. These hoes is thirsty."

It suddenly began making sense why some of the women were a bit more friendly than usual and why they were offering to help Judah with various things, including bringing by a meal or babysitting the children.

"Where would they get an idea like that?" asked Judah. "Dee and I are real good. That's just how we flow. She's in her element right now and letting me sort out this stuff."

"You're good but she walks around here mad at the world, sulking, don't want to be bothered and your mother makes certain we all know that she is no good to you nor is she good for you," Alphonso pointed out. "Like she's holding auditions for a future daughter-in-law. If I were you, I would have a trusted family friend or advisor give Derika the heads up so she is prepared to handle First Lady. You and I both know your mother does not handle competition well and she will pull down whoever is in her way."

"I don't know what to do about them anymore," Judah shook his head in disbelief. "Daddy had a way of keeping everyone at peace." "You the head of the house now," Alphonso told him. "The same way Christ is head of the church, the husband is head of the house. Either you going to protect her, or you going to let your mother take her. Keep in mind, I like her a lot so don't mess it up."

Lavinia had been playing the role of doting grandmother to her grandchildren and ensuring Judah was happy and comfortable. He found himself escaping to his brother's house for a few minutes to get away from her. He just sat on the couch or porch like they used to and think. He avoided going into the nursery that already had Hope's pictures on the wall and in Josiah and Rachel's bedroom that still had a few things scattered as they were last-minute packers.

"And while I have your attention, I want to talk to you about Maya," Alphonso continued not realizing that Judah was in his trance. "Your mini-me has something special. She can sang! I would like her to sit in and practice with us. But not JJ. That child has absolutely no talent for music and First Lady needs to stop pressuring me to give him a lead. If I give him a mic, Black Jesus will come down from that painting and revoke our choir card. Judah, are you listening?"

"Yeah… I am," Judah said staring at the musicians.

Alphonso saw a glimmer of the sad little boy who was just itching to find out how things worked. He noticed Judah before Judah noticed himself and told Lavinia to let the boys attend youth choir practice. It was a 'no' as Lavinia already had her sons in training to lead the church the day they were born and the music ministry was not the place for them. Josiah told Alphonso that Judah could play all the songs the choir sang even though he couldn't read music. When the keyboardist got sick on a Sunday morning, Josiah told Darold that Judah knew the songs and sure enough, he played the piano as if he had years of training and later revealed he had an excellent command of the drums and guitar as well. When Alphonso walked in on Judah singing to himself, he told Darold that he was willing to nurture what he described as a rare gift that was destined to go global.

"This is my practice, not a jam session," Alphonso sighed. "You itching like a dog in a dinosaur museum. Go on. It'll be good for everyone and get your mind off whatever it is you are thinking about. Can't fool me."

Judah smiled as he received permission to hang out with the choir. He sat down to the keyboard and pulled a mic to his mouth.

"Y'all ready?" he smiled.

Two of the women took a step closer to Judah. Alphonso walked in front of them and dramatically flipped his scarf to warn them to back up. As Judah got everyone hyped, Alphonso decided to take it upon himself to warn Derika that she was about to get a rude awakening if she didn't hurry home and woman up to face Lavinia and the church.

Derika returned just in time for the updates from various ministries. She sat quietly in her seat as she listened to the reports. Her phone suddenly went off disrupting service. Of course, Lavinia gave her a look of disapproval while Judah found it amusing.

"You're back in Atl," a message came through on her phone. "I'm signing with you. Cam."

"Stop," she responded before putting her phone on silent.

"Don't make me pull up again D," he replied.

Derika put the phone in her handbag and turned her attention to Fiona who was now speaking.

"If you all can find it in your hearts to sow a seed to the missionary fund, it will complete the work started by Bishop Josiah and Sis. Rachel," Fiona addressed the rather bored congregation. "And finally, the women's ministry has raised over twenty-thousand dollars for this project and some of that is going to the shelter we need to be built by winter when families are at their most vulnerable. The shelter will be able to house ten families facing hard times. So if you can't give, we need you to join the mission, family and women's ministries or at least make a pledge in order for us to hit that five-million-dollar mark."

"Thank you for that Sis. Fiona," Judah said standing in an attempt to liven up the crowd. "We appreciate all the work you do."

"And we appreciate you, Bishop," Fiona nodded. "Rachel served in so many ways as Bishop Josiah's wife. It takes a woman of a certain caliber to lead us and we are honored to continue what she started."

Lavinia chuckled under her breath as some of the women glanced at Derika unapprovingly. Derika took a deep breath and tried her best to ignore them. She felt her phone vibrate in her purse and looked to see who it was.

"Perhaps a few words from First Lady?" Fiona suggested to Judah.

"Absolutely!" Judah agreed.

Lavinia gracefully stood and tilted her head as she received applause.

"Thank you!" Derika said as she walked towards the stage. "Thank you so much. You are too kind!"

Lavinia and Fiona exchanged glances as Paul helped Derika up and she walked over to Fiona. Shay and Alphonso sat up, rather amused and hoping for a little exchange. Judah prepared himself for whatever his mother was about to say and looked up at the sound booth to indicate to them to be prepared to mute the microphones.

"I meant -" Fiona stammered looking at Lavinia.

"I find that term First Lady so unapproachable don't you agree?" Derika asked the congregation as she took a mic. "I personally don't like the term so 'Derika' is fine, 'Dee' is even better. I know I've been a little busy trying to balance everything, but Greater Gates, I am a part of this family too. I don't say much but I have to speak on this. Fiona, I admire you ladies who are able to raise families, be immaculate wives, balance your career, look fabulous every Sunday and still give tirelessly to the work of the Lord. My sister-in-law, she was that kind of woman. Can I get an amen?"

"Amen!" the congregation agreed.

"That being said, I would like to propose we name the shelter Rachel's Refuge in her honor as she was most deserving. And to those precious orphans and my little niece Hope who they never got to bring to her new home, I propose we name the new orphanage The Hope House."

"I concur!" Paul shouted as others applauded.

"And... I know my husband complains about my spending but I'm going to spend a little bit more right now, and answer to Bishop later," Derika glanced at Judah who was thoroughly enjoying whatever it was she was doing.

"That's alright sister girl!" a woman shouted.

"I'm going to dip into our personal finances and match what you have raised so far," Derika handed Fiona a credit card. "So that's twenty-thousand from you, twenty-thousand from us and if everyone in here can give just twenty dollars, I think we will be able to at least complete the first phase of ensuring those families can stay together. And Sis. Fiona, I was invited to an event with some powerful ladies who are movers and shakers in the city and would be honored if you can come and present your work. Your labor in the vineyard has not gone unnoticed."

Derika hugged Fiona as Lavinia sat back down, boiling mad but with a smile. She clapped politely.

"Lord have mercy, she done pulled a Lavinia on Lavinia," Alphonso said quietly as he fanned himself. "Giving me hot flashes in here."

Judah gave Derika a nod of approval as he quickly squeezed her hand.

"I'd like to match that by donating one million dollars and inviting the youth to a game night," they saw a hand go up in the back.

"Who said that?" Alphonso put his fan above his eyes. "Somebody done robbed King Solomon's mines?"

"It's Cameron Diggs!" Shay squealed to the girls sitting beside her. "I met him when we were in LA!"

Phones went up to take photos and videos of Cameron as he strolled up to the front. He and Judah shook hands as everyone chatted excitedly.

"They've turned this church into a circus," Lavinia shook her head. "Paul, you see why I said she is not right for Greater Gates?"

"That's Cam Diggs!" Paul told her. "That boy can play!"

"Cameron Diggs, now did you say what I think you said?" Judah asked.

"I said one million and a game night on me," Cameron repeated. "So thank you to my new manager, Ms. Dee for giving me the heads up on this wonderful cause and when y'all come out, I'll be sure our team's foundation knows too so you come on out Ms. Fiona get a lil something extra."

Fiona giggled excitedly as she held Derika's hand.

"Cam, would you mind taking a photo for our social media page?" Derika asked Fiona giggled.

"No problem at all," Cameron said standing between them as Derika went to sit back down. "Anything for my new manager."

"Derika, come on," Fiona whispered.

"No girl, that's your hard work and your moment!" Derika said. "Pastor Jones, you go in too."

Paul smiled and went to stand with them as the church's media team went to work. Derika crossed her legs and ran her fingers across her hair as she looked at Lavinia.

"You want to fight fire with fire?" Lavinia said to herself. "Nobody upstages me in my house. Game on Delilah."

CHAPTER 12

Derika overheard Judah telling Darold what occurred later on and smiled as she listened to Barbara ask for more details. She peeked and watched Judah help Barbara get Darold cleaned up and saw how gentle he was as he helped.

"Now Judah, I'm not trying to get in your business, but your wife sounds like she really has your back," Barbara said. "You're a lucky man."

"I am," Judah said. "Daddy was real good at talking to us about being good husbands and fathers. Valuable lessons."

"She made some soup for your father," Barbara told him. "She said maybe the smell will wake him up."

"Yeah?" Judah laughed. "Only Dee would think to bring a man being kept alive by machines soup. I'm a be real with you, she can't cook that well but she sure as hell knows how to make a good soup like her grandmother did. Now them oxtails you made the other day, I'd wake up for that!"

"If I mind you, you'll have me bursting with giggles all day," she laughed. "You are a good son. Most people would put a man like this in hospice but you are so hands-on it's amazing. I wish Mrs. Waters had the time."

"She makes time for what she wants," Judah sighed knowing that Barbara meant his mother. "Hey Daddy... you believe how long it's been since I've been on the road? You want me to tell you about the song I was thinking of recording?"

Derika took a deep breath as she stepped away from the door.

"God or Jesus or whoever, I don't ask you for a lot of things or even talk to you," Derika prayed quietly. "But I ask you to please let Darold come back to Judah. They need each other. They really need each other. So please, give them that."

Derika heard a door open and saw Lavinia watching her.

"You are a cunning little snake, avoiding me these past few days," Lavinia said as she walked nearby. "You try a stunt like what you pulled again, I will see to it that you get what you deserve."

"Judah…" Derika called, pretending to ignore Lavinia.

"What's up?" he asked, stepping out of the room.

"I'm craving fries real bad," she wrapped her arms around his waist.

"You want me to bring you something?"

"I can come with you," he offered.

"I don't want you to come just in case your dad wakes up," she looked back to the room. "I think he's almost awake."

"Thanks babe," he said. "Wait, you're not pregnant are you? Last time you were in that fries craze it was Maya."

"Well it's not like we're on the road," she kissed him.

"Cut it out!" Lavinia said. "I don't need to see all that and Darold does not need to wake up to it! Always all over each other."

"I'll be back soon," Derika said, kissing him again. "I'll call you from the window."

"Miss you already," he said as she walked past Lavinia.

"Respect my house," Lavinia warned him when Derika left. "All that touching and grabbing and holding and headboard banging."

"She's my wife," he shrugged. "And you know there is no headboard banging. We don't do that."

"She's a witch!" Lavinia said. "Just stop all that kissing and touching in front of me. I don't trust her. Mark my word, you are going to end up in a ditch because of her. While you are young and someone is willing to take on two adorable stepchildren, I suggest you leave her."

"Mama…" Judah sighed and turned to go back in the room to Darold.

"Judah…" Lavinia said. "You need to prepare to let him go. Do not prolong him from receiving his heavenly reward."

Judah shut the door and picked up a bible to read to Darold. Barbara quietly slipped out to give them privacy.

A short time later and a few miles away, Derika opened the roof of her SUV to allow fresh air in as she drove through the city. She made her way downtown and a highrise condo caught her eye. She decided her fries would wait and went to make an unannounced visit, banging on the door of one of the luxury units until it opened.

"Cameron Diggs, you want to get benched with an injury off the court?" Derika asked when he let her in his condo.

"I'm guessing the check cleared?" he asked. "You ain't got to barge in with an attitude. I'm doing great, thank you for asking."

"How in the hell do you show up at church dropping a million dollars, inviting them out to the game and telling people I'm your manager?" Derika turned and folded her arms.

"You made me resort to this," he told her, going into his phone. "You want a direct deposit?"

"I have not offered you shit!" she said. "I have people calling me asking me info on you as if I rep you."

"And what are you doing about it?" asked Cameron.

"I arranged for Ruby, my partner, to get a team to handle it," she sighed, realizing that by saying she took care of setting him up, she would be proving his point that she was amazing at what she did.

"That's my girl," he smiled.

"But I am just advising, not managing," she pointed a finger at him. "And learn boundaries. Don't drop by my house again and stay your ass up out of my husband's church. Move."

"Nah," he leaned against the door. "You over here. We might as well chill for a bit."

"Move!" she repeated.

"Move me," he dared her. "You short women always have the biggest attitude."

"I'm not short," she rolled her eyes.

"You short to me," he stooped down.

"You're not even funny," she told him.

"You don't like me because I'm funny," he said, running his hands up her thighs then pulling her closer to him as he felt her hips. "Or did you forget why you like me?"

"Cameron…" Derika pushed against him.

"Calling my name already?" he asked, pulling up her skirt while making himself more comfortable.

"You need to stop," she warned him, feeling his lips on her skin. "Just…"

"Shh…" he said, pulling her lace panties to the side while putting one of her legs over his shoulder.

She inhaled deeply, her mouth opening slightly when she felt him find what he was looking for with his tongue. Her handbag fell beside him as she put a hand against the door behind him to balance. She threw her head back and bit her bottom lip as he teased her by flickering her lightly as he traced the inner lips of her most intimate parts. She removed her blazer, suddenly feeling extremely hot. He stopped for a moment to pick her up and take her to the couch, exchanging kisses with her as he did. As they shed their clothes, he turned on some music to set even more of a mood. Cameron enjoyed pursuing her and wearing her down. It would take him a few weeks to do so but once he got her to submit, she thoroughly enjoyed their entanglement.

"I haven't been touched like that in so long…" she whispered between breaths as he moved his head more vigorously between her legs.

She reached down to touch his head as he reached up to fondle her nipple with one hand and inserted two fingers in her. She felt his lips grip tighter, seemingly sucking the life out of her while somehow resuscitating the neglected woman within her. She arched her back as the feeling took over her, settling in her loins and forcing her to wildly explode.

"Damn girl," he said, wiping his mouth. "That's some sweet shit right there."

He pulled her to the edge of the couch.

"Hold up…" she stopped him. "We're not playing that game."

"I got you," he got a condom from his pants pocket.

"So you knew I was coming over here and this was going to happen?" she asked as he put it on.

"Don't it eventually always happen though?" he slid it down over his erection. "I don't know why you try to delay it because it happens. Come here. Fuck Dee, how come you stay so sweet?"

She held onto him as he helped get rid of all the stresses she accumulated recently. She loved how he spoke to her, telling her how sexy she was. She loved how he wanted to see himself sliding in and out of her while her breasts bounced. She loved knowing she could spend the next week feeling his sensation. They had undeniable chemistry, each thoroughly fulfilled with the other. They moved their activities from the main area and the kitchen counter before the bedroom.

Cameron settled to get comfortable for the rest of the night. He was puzzled when she got up and began getting dressed.

"You really going to leave?" he asked, pulling her close to kiss her again.

"I have a family to go home to," she reminded him.

"Why you do me like that?" Cameron asked. "You know I like you right?"

"Cam… your star is rising," Derika pulled back. "You need only your career. Not a woman to distract you."

"You're a woman," he reached for her again. "A hell of a lot of woman."

"A married woman," she reminded him.

"Can't be that good a marriage if you be meeting up with me," Cameron said. "That man so caught up in his hallelujah I bet he don't even know how to handle your fine ass."

"Cameron, you are too young for me," she laughed. "You're not even thirty yet."

"You need a young buck not a middle-aged boring churchman," he leaned in to kiss her.

"Don't be disrespecting him to me and still go to him for counseling," Derika turned from him. "That's another thing. Terminate that. You can't be talking to him like that. He was just being courteous after your donation. You were supposed to say no and not show up."

"Nah," he laughed. "He offers good advice. Good solid advice. Bet he can't give me advice on dealing with you though. He going to blink and you be gone. You and them kids. Tell him fuck up and I'll step up."

"My son is not listening to someone ten to fifteen years older than him as a stepdad," Derika told him. "No way in hell. You need to find someone younger and single. This needs to stop."

Cameron watched her fix her hair.

"What about that girl who was by you last time I went to your house in California?" he asked. "She's like eighteen right?"

"See, you even think like a boy not a man," she scoffed. "First of all she's like my child and second, she will never be a ho' for the likes of y'all. Get your life together. I'm grown. Your petty threats don't mean shit to me."

"Stay the night," Cameron begged her again.

"Not happening," she said walking to the door. "And stay your ass from around my husband and his church."

"Don't make me have to get your attention again," he kissed her before opening the door for her.

"Approach me properly next time and respect my family," she reminded him. "Ruby will be sending over your contract and my retainer is non-refundable."

"Well you better put in there that I need two hours twice a week to meet," he kissed her again.

"Do not push it," she said. "And work on your rebounds. That last game had some silly mistakes you should not have made."

CHAPTER 13

Against her better judgment, Derika continued to see Cameron and it actually made her tolerate Judah more. He was a sweet escape from the pressures Lavinia gave and the lack of interest Judah showed lately. Judah left early and came in late, and the time he did spend at home, he spent with Darold or the children when he wasn't sleeping. Their conversations were cordial greetings instead of affection or sking the other's opinion in problem solving. He made it easy for her to seek affections elsewhere and didnt seem to notice her that she was going out a lot ore often. Whenever Derika peeped in on Judah, he had his headphones on and seemed as if he did not want to be bothered. Then there were nights where he would be agitated for no reason and make a mess of his side of the closet until he calmed down. Derika learned to sit quietly and let him be. He would eventually slide in bed with her and drift off.

After a full day that included meetings, lunch with the women, catching up with Cameron and then an evening with the children, Derika was fast asleep when she heard Judah rummaging through the closet and drawers.

"Why aren't you in bed?" she asked. "Do you see what time it is? You need to rest."

"Dee…" Judah called desperately. "Were you in my drawer?"

"Why?" Derika asked from their bed.

"I had a shirt… I mean a shaving kit," he said. "You saw it?"

"No," she said. "But I did tell JJ he can go in your drawer. He wanted a watch or something. He took it."

"Fuck!" Judah said quietly.

"What's wrong?" Derika asked.

"Where is he?" Judah seemed to panic.

"I think he's at a sleepover," Derika watched him get frustrated then got up.

"You think?" Judah asked, pacing the floor. "My children do not do sleepovers! Where is he really?"

"Sleeping like he should be and you're not going to wake him up to ask him about bags of coke and heroin and oxy that shouldn't be in the house in the first place," Derika told him.

Judah rubbed his hands together and looked at her. He saw the disappointment on her face.

"Big Saturday night, you got a sermon in the morning but you need your little shaving kit to concentrate?" she asked. "I was looking for the oils to get my anxiety down and try to sleep. Imagine what I found."

"Where are they?" Judah demanded.

"You promised me Judah," Derika reminded him. "You promised you would never touch it again after you nearly drowned them."

"I never would harm my children!" he objected.

"I'm sorry," Derika corrected herself. "You were just trying to baptize them in the pool in the middle of the night? Thank goodness you triggered the alarm doing shit because you could've killed them! You're lucky they thought it was a game and they were able to swim."

Judah barely remembered that night. That was the night Ruby insisted Derika stop enabling him and to acknowledge he had become a danger.

"You can't do this by yourself," Ruby had told her once the children were back in their beds. "Call his brother and y'all fix this. He is about to lose his career and life messing with that. I'm happy you called me but suppose you weren't here? Those children would've. Addiction is a serious illness Derika."

"I'm done," Derika let herself cry. I just saw them on the monitor."

"Call his brother," Derika said. "Time to check him into rehab again."

That was the closest they had come to separating. Judah looked at her and sighed.

"Dee… I had it to remind me not to do it," he told her. "Just give it back."

Derika hugged Judah and he returned it. She ran her hands down his shoulders and arms and then stopped. He suddenly realized what she was doing and pulled back.

"Show me," she told him. "Show me your arms. Or are you doing it between your toes again? Take off your shoes."

He stood silent without a fight.

"Seriously?" she shook her head.

"I just need it in a very small dose to concentrate," he whispered when she saw the discolored patch on his skin. "I don't get high."

"Suppose JJ found it and ingested it?" Derika stepped back with tears in her eyes. "Gave it to Maya and they played with it? Would you rather they die or get taken away? Answer me Bishop Waters. I lied for you. Ruby lied for you. I said I was done when you hid it in Maya's diapers on the plane. I said I was done and still put up with you and you can't even commit to a plan."

"Don't you dare throw that diaper thing in my face," he told her. "This is not my lane and I just can't handle it."

"So concede, give this up and let's work on getting you better," she shrugged. "Give it up and let's go home."

"I need to be near my dad," he said.

"You need to be making responsible choices as a dad," she told him. "Judah, if people knew this side…"

"You have sides too," Judah reminded her.

"Fine," she said, stepping closer to him. "Then you can tell Shay how you got her father killed. Marco Sanchez was in and out of jail because of you. He died and left a little girl who barely got to know him behind because you wanted that last hit, and he took you to his supplier. He went to go get it for you. They shot him down because of you. And here you here breaking a promise to him, his child, me, your children and your brother yet again. You really need to be high to preach? That's not ethical nor is it right."

Derika saw the tears in Judah's eyes. It was the one secret she kept from Shay; she respected Judah had to be the one to tell her.

"I think it's best you head back to L.A for a minute," Judah told Derika.

"Judah I'm sorry but you forced me to say it," Derika sighed. "I'm so tired of fighting. We never used to fight like this. It's this environment we're in. Come with me. Take a break and come."

Judah heard her words but her bringing up Marco stung.

"Derika, support me or separate yourself from me," he said walking to the bathroom. "Just put my shit back."

"The fuck?" she gasped. "Oh. It's like that. I'm supposed to put your shit back but ignore the real issue?"

"Yeah," he said. "It's like that."

"Here…" she held up two of the bags and a syringe she had in her pocket.

"You play too damn much," he said, returning to her.

Just as he reached for them, she ripped them open, spilling the contents to the floor. Judah got on his knees to try scoop it up. Derika watched him for a moment and took out her phone. Judah looked up at her and realized she was recording him.

"Give me that!" he tried grabbing it from her.

"No!" she pushed him back. "You see what it makes you become? You've been back on it and hiding! You are a liar and you're unfit!"

"Derika give me the damn phone!" Judah grabbed her arm.

"Don't you touch me!" she punched him hard enough to make him let her go.

"Give me the goddamn phone!" he demanded, grabbing her. "Derika, you got me pissed off now!"

"Do you see what it makes you become?" she said, struggling to pull back. "Judah, you are hurting me! Stop it! If you don't quit I will scream!"

"You had no right moving my shit!" he tried prying the phone from her hands.

They were both startled when the bedroom door swung open and Lavinia barged in with a baseball bat.

"There's a sick man and sleeping children in this house!" she told them. "Not to mention staff who can't wait to break an NDA if the gossip is good enough. What the hell is going on?"

Lavinia saw the bags and syringes on the floor.

"Girl, what kind of ignorance and sin you bringing into my house?" Lavinia demanded. "And turn off that damn phone. Don't you ever record within my home!"

Derika looked at Judah and he let her go.

"Just a misunderstanding, Mama," Judah said. "We'll keep it down."

"What did you do to him?" Lavinia asked Derika. "Answer me, girl!"

"Lavinia…" Derika's eyes began filling with tears as she took a deep breath. "Your son has a problem and you need to get him help. I have done this before and I'm not able to handle everything on top of this. I am done with him."

"Well it's about time!" Lavinia raised a hand to heaven. "Right on time, Lord! Ten years of praying and you have not forsaken my prayer! He could've done so much better. So much better."

"Lavinia, the way I feel right now I will bust a bitch so do not fuck with me!" Derika warned.

"Make sure you get custody and if you need me to testify against her, I will," Lavina looked at Derika while speaking to Judah. "Make it official after ordination because I done paid for all that stuff. You can leave Sunday night after the reception."

Derika waited for Judah to correct Lavinia and defend her. He said nothing. She shook her head.

"Judah, I need you out of this bedroom please," Derika told him.

"Little girl, this is my house and my son," Lavinia reminded her. "The husband is the head of the house as Christ is the head of the church. You fall in line. If anyone needs to leave it's you."

"You see how big he is compared to me?" Derika asked Lavinia. "You strut in here and see his hands on me and yet it's my fault?"

"My boys were raised properly," Lavinia said. "Two-parent, God-fearing household where they were taught to respect all. Whatever you did to provoke him is on you."

"Mama…" Judah sighed. "We'll keep it down."

"Fine," Derika said walking into their closet. "Then stay. Both of you."

Judah picked up the items from the floor and put them on a nightstand.

"Grow a backbone!" Lavinia told him. "You've always been so soft. Don't let her talk to you like that in your house. The nerve of her. Josiah would never let any of those chicken heads disrespect him. The way you let her run your career and your house is not natural. Lead, son!"

"Mama, maybe you ought to give us a moment," Judah sighed, sitting on the bed. "This is between us."

"Judah, I have always known what was best for you and that girl has been your biggest disappointment to date," Lavinia said. "The only thing she did right was those two children and she still went about that incorrectly intentionally getting pregnant while you were climbing the gospel charts. Mother knows best and she is not a wife to represent a man of God. Legally separate then divorce."

Derika reemerged with a saucy wig and a tight dress with a plunging neckline. She went to Judah's nightstand and took out two credit cards.

"The whore of Babylon in the flesh," Lavinia put her hand over her chest. "Ass and titties out for the world to see! Lewd! Judah, see, I told you this woman ain't nothing but lewd! What kind of mother waltzes out of the house this close to midnight in something that covers less than a bikini?"

"One who knows where to go to be appreciated when she's no longer needed at home," Derika grabbed her makeup bag.

She reached for another bag from her side of the bed. Judah knew the private contents it contained and couldn't hold back.

"This has gone too far," he told her. "I know you ain't going out, nowhere, especially with… with that."

"Apologize," Derika stopped and looked at Judah.

"You owe me an apology!" he seemed surprised she wanted him to go first. "I owe you?"

"She needs to owe you for that oversized vehicle you got her -" Lavinia began but stopped when she got a look from Judah.

"You going to apologize to me for what you did?" Judah asked Derika.

Derika put a hand up and walked by him, disappointed in his actions.

"Don't you leave this house in that dress before you ruin our reputation!" Lavinia spoke up. "Judah, you need to man up and put your foot down."

"Apologize to me Judah," Derika repeated as she put her hand on the door.

Judah scratched the side of his face and turned his head. Derika knew he wasn't apologizing to her. She turned and walked out the door.

"Judah, don't let her go out looking like that!" Lavinia told him.

"She's going to drive around then come to her senses," he shrugged.

Over three hours later, Lavinia walked into the study to find Judah listening to music while reading.

"You got her to calm down yet?" Lavinia asked, turning down the music.

"I'm sure she's upstairs still angry at me," Judah closed his bible.

"She sure looks angry," Lavinia handed him her phone.

Judah clenched his jaw when he saw a photo of Derika mingling at a reality show mixer with a rapper's hand on her waist and his eyes on her breasts. He was even more annoyed to see her with a glass in her hand as she sat with Cameron who had his arm around her.

"Twenty people sent me photos noticing how Bishop Judah's wife is all gussied up like a tramp," Lavinia said. "This girl is about to bring down four generations of hard work and divine favor in this family. Judah, I want her gone. Either you deal with her, or I shall."

By the time Derika strolled in, it was almost dawn. She met Judah sitting on the bed on his laptop.

"I hope you were not driving drunk," Judah told her.

"Cameron and his driver were nice enough to make sure I got home," she said, trying to gather her words.

She smiled to herself thinking of how she tossed Maya's car seat aside, pulled up her dress and used Cameron to get rid of her frustrations with Judah in the back seat before he drove her and his driver drove behind them.

"Crisis PR costs a lot of money these days," Judah told her as she took off her shoes and climbed into bed. "They are spinning it that you're Cameron's manager and you are trying to get him a TV deal. Ruby came up with that one and it's actually pretty good. Go take a shower. I smelled the liquor on you from you entered the room."

"What's wrong?" she slurred. "I already know not to rely on you to protect me. You don't protect me from your mother. You don't protect me from them church bitches. You didn't protect me that night. You are a fucking fail. And you sing through your nose and don't enunciate properly. You sound the way you do because you keep putting that shit up your system. You're lucky you know how to engineer that crap out."

"You're drunk Derika," he looked at her. "You're drunk and I have a team cleaning up this stuff before it gets leaked further. This whole internet scrubbing thing is not easy. You have no idea what you are about to cause happen to us."

"Judah…" Derika took off her wig. "Shut up. Just shut the fuck up."

"You better be up in an hour to get breakfast together and the children in order," he told her.

"I'm going to sleep this off," Derika told him. "Take care of your own damn kids."

"I have to go over these notes from Paul," Judah said.

"What that got to do with me?" she asked. "Shut up. I'm tired."

"Two hours and I'm waking you up," Judah told her.

Lavinia tried to smile at church as people asked her if Derika was alright. Derika quickly drove off and left the children to Lavinia and Judah. Lavinia picked them up from children's church and noticed JJ was just as grumpy as Derika appeared to be.

"Why is your smile upside down?" she asked him. "The Lord loves us to be cheerful."

"First Lady!" one of the directors called to her.

"What's wrong with my grandson?" Lavinia asked.

"He's a little disappointed," she replied. "We were casting roles for the church play and well, I didn't give him a singing part."

"Don't you know who his father is?" Lavinia asked. "He's been around music his whole life. You need to give him a singing part."

"The little girl, now she has a singing part," she explained. "In fact, she has most of the solo parts. She can sing and she understands the music keys and she picks up very well when it comes to the keyboard. I think your grandson however may have a different calling. And if music is not his passion then we need to allow him to tell us what he would like to do."

"That is absolutely ridiculous," Lavinia laughed, glancing at JJ chatting with some of the boys. "Everyone in my family was very musically inclined. You probably haven't found his voice."

"God bless his heart but he cannot sing if it would save his life," she told Lavinia. "I wouldn't have known that was Judah's child unless you had told me. He looks more like his mother's family anyway. I suppose he got her talents as well as her looks."

Lavinia looked at JJ a bit more closely, concerned that he might be picking up Derika's habits.

"Well, we can't fault him for her genetics," Lavina smiled. "I'll make sure he and Maya practice."

Lavina walked to the car with the children. She watched JJ help Maya in her booster seat and thought of how Derika and her family were likely the reason JJ missed the music skills.

"That girl runs everything," Lavinia muttered to herself.

"What you say Grandma?" Maya asked.

"I was just praying baby," she smiled. "I heard you sang so well today. Your daddy is going to be so proud. I bet you're going to be an excellent singer just like him with hit records."

"Mommy says we're not going to be singers," Maya said matter-of-factly. "She says we're going to be normal and not be industry babies."

"Your mother is basic and doesn't know any better," Lavinia said. "You will sing and JJ will preach."

"Nope!" JJ shook his head. "I'm going to play basketball like Cam Diggs. He told me I can come to his camp and he can teach me himself."

"Oh did he?" Lavinia laughed. "Did you go to his game?"

"No," JJ said pulling out his phone to play a game. "He comes by our real house. I mean the LA house."

"Your father didn't mention he was friends with Cameron," Lavinia said.

"He's Mom's friend," JJ said. "I don't think he knows Daddy."

"He doesn't know Daddy because only him and Mommy talk in her office for the meeting," Maya added. "We're not supposed to interrupt Mommy. She's very busy making all our lives easier."

"Oh?" Lavinia raised her eyebrows. "How about we go have some crab legs and then I take you for ice cream? But don't tell your parents. It'll be our secret."

"Okay!" JJ beamed as Maya clapped.

"We'll go as soon as I am done at the pharmacy," Lavinia said. "I forgot I have to pick up a prescription. You two can stay in the car for that."

CHAPTER 14

Paul noticed the body language between Derika and Judah as they sat in Judah's office on a sofa. He'd also noticed the tension and distance that was developing between them from the forced smiles to not holding hands in public and not even a thank you at dinner.

"So in this past hour, have we learned to be less hostile with each other?" Paul asked them.

"Pastor Jones, I'm sorry but I think you're wasting your time," Derika told him. "Don't get me wrong, I really like you and appreciate everything you have done. But at the same time, Josiah was the only one he trusted enough to offer spiritual advising or marital counseling. That's because Josiah saw and knew all the bullshit."

"We are in a church," Paul reminded her.

"It's a building Paul," Derika said. "Yall act like God actually lives in here. It's four walls that can come down at any moment. God doesn't save his people nor have mercy on children who already lost parents and lived in poverty. He kills them, infants and all."

"Derika, are you still grieving over what happened?" Paul asked.

"Rachel and Josiah were people," Derika replied. "They were our people and y'all just move on like… I'm fine. We can move on."

Derika looked around the room, with its modern style and traditional finishes. She saw a picture of Rachel and Josiah on a desk and turned her head.

"Bishop, do you have anything you want to say?" Paul asked Judah.

"I'm sorry," Judah said. "I'll try to be better."

"What are you sorry for?" Paul asked.

"She knows," Judah said quietly.

Paul tried to hide a smile, knowing that Judah only said he was sorry to appease Derika. He could tell that he didn't even remember why she was upset with him.

"Even if you two are not happy, around here, you better look it," Paul said. "I need you to attempt a conversation as friends first. Then we can work on the marriage part. Is that something we can do? Don't make me have to fuss y'all. Hold hands and agree to it."

Judah and Derika reluctantly held hands. It was the first time in about two weeks they had done so.

"Bishop, why don't you suggest something you would like for Derika to consider to help ease the burden from you?" Paul coaxed him.

"Derika, I think you need to be a part of these women's events so you can learn how to socialize and act properly," Judah said.

"Well I think you need to find yourself a friend and stop relying on friendship from me," Derika said.

"I don't keep friends here," Judah said. "I don't need friends here. All my friends are out west. My last real friend here was Marco and I am not having friends here all up in my business."

"Well I can't deal with you alone," Derika said. "You need male energy."

"I just need a spouse who supports me," he said. "I can't even talk to you about how I feel. I lived in that house and in this church with someone I can't ever get back. I would love to handle it but it's hard and you make it harder."

"Everything I do is to accommodate you though," Derika said. "When are you going to accommodate me?"

"When you put away childish things and act like an adult," Judah told her. "Grow up Derika."

Paul sighed and looked at them holding hands but disconnected emotionally.

"Pastor Jones?" Judah's receptionist peered in. "Your next appointment is already in your office."

"Thank you, Michelle," Judah said grateful for the distraction.

"Oh that's the city council representative," Paul got up. "Y'all stop this nonsense and work it out, please. In fact, hold hands and count to one hundred. I'll be back shortly."

Judah and Derika complied, eventually relaxing a bit with each other.

"You seem like you're glowing," Judah said, breaking the silence. "Something happening I should know about?"

"I haven't seen your mother for the day," Derika replied. "That usually makes me radiant."

They both chuckled.

"You make me so mad, I want to slap you," Derika admitted. "Only reason I don't do it is because you'd probably enjoy it."

"Yeah," he confessed. "I would enjoy it."

They laughed. She rested her head on his shoulder and sighed. They sat together for a moment. He patted her leg and got up to sit at his desk.

"Well, we tried," Derika shrugged.

"I'm good, just a little busy Dee," he said, picking up a file of papers he had next to him. "I have a ton of stuff to approve before the convention. When you leave, I have this, Daddy and the kids. It's a lot. Meetings, sessions, I barely get a break. So if you have to leave…"

"Please Judah, just enjoy the moment," she said, sitting on his lap and resting her head on his shoulder again. "Just one more minute."

Judah sighed and put down his papers. He missed her smell. That sweet yet sophisticated fragrance she wore and the honey and berries from her hair products. They both felt better when he put his arms around her.

"Can I ask you something?" Derika spoke up.

"Of course," he said, somewhat happy they were at least communicating again.

"What could I do that would make you file for divorce?" she asked. "I understand your mother is running her mouth but I needed to ask you what can I do to expedite it if that's what you really want."

Derika looked up at him.

"Absolutely nothing and I never said I wanted to break up," he said. "We get mad with each other and we work it out. Why would you even think that we should get divorced? It's just my duty is here and I know you miss LA. You always come back reenergized and happy. I can't give you what you truly desire yet but I will try."

"When this is over, we will get back to our life and move on and not visit for a year," she said.

Judah sighed and looked at her. She knew he was building up courage to tell her something.

"Dee... I've... I've been asked to stay on," Judah told her. "It's been more than six months and they like the growth. Honestly, I'm starting to adjust and the kids are doing great in school."

"Judah... I married you not this," Derika said calmly in an attempt not to yell at him. "I committed to you, not Greater Gates. What did you tell them?"

"I told them I have to pray on it," Judah replied.

"You can't even tell them you have to talk to your wife first?" Derika asked. "That's right. The husband is the head of the house according to Greater Gates. I used to like our equal partnership style marriage. That used to make me feel like we mattered to each other. Remember when you would help me with the children and I would help you with everything?"

Judah took a deep breath wondering why Derika was making everything so hard as of late.

"Derika I came to you before saying yes and I still get no credit," Judah pointed out. "I value you which is why I brought it to the table."

"Judah... it's either us or this church," she said firmly. "I'm sorry. I know my limitations and I can't do this anymore. I tried. I adjusted. I'm not happy. If you do this permanently, you will not have me by your side."

"After all we have gone through, you'd walk?" he asked. "And where would the children be?"

"You have the power to ensure it never gets to that," she put a finger to his lips.

They stared at each other for a moment. He kissed her forehead just as the door opened.

"Judah I was thinking -" Lavinia walked in without knocking. "This is a church, not some couple's motel suite."

"I was just leaving," Derika stood up and reached for her handbag. To further aggravate Lavinia, she leaned over and took her time in kissing Judah, then wiped her lipstick off his lips and straightened his collar. She kissed him again.

"If you've quite finished!" Lavinia clapped her hands.

"I'll see you at home, Lavinia," Dericka nodded as she walked by her.

"First Lady Waters while here please," Lavinia told her.

"Yes ma'am Mother Waters," Derika said.

"Mother?" Lavinia gasped. "Do I look like I'm celebrating my centennial?"

"First Lady is normally used for the wife of the most senior Bishop," Derika mused. "Mother is used for the seniors so I thought -"

"Dee I'll call you when I'm on the way home," Judah interrupted her from his desk, tickled that she could be so upset with him but still do what she did if it meant aggravating Lavinia.

"You need to put her in her place," Lavinia told him as soon as Derika closed the door.

"Mama she got you good on that one though," Judah laughed.

"This is a place of business and the Lord's work," Lavinia opened her hands to indicate the sacredness of the church. "She needs to sit in a chair, not on your lap."

"You should've knocked," Judah smiled. "You keep walking in on us and being disrespectful."

Lavinia shook her head as she took a seat.

"I heard you're being asked to accept the official role of bishop," Lavinia smiled proudly. "You proved yourself and I am delighted that you stepped up. I wanted to find out if you wanted to have the reception at the hotel or the house."

"Mama, we haven't decided if I'm accepting the offer yet," Judah got back into his paperwork.

"We?" Lavinia repeated. "Son, there is no we. You accept it."

"I have to think about what's best for my family," he said.

"I am your family," Lavinia told him. "Your brother was your family. This church is your family. We were there before her and we will be after her. See... you young people rush and let your loins choose instead of waiting to see if you're equally yoked. That girl has never been a church girl. Who knows how they raised her. Thank goodness her grandmother tried but baby it wasn't good enough and you know it. Look at Fiona Prescott. Or Andrea. Niesha. All raised properly and excellent church wives who understand the task. The best of that generation was Rachel. Now, Rachel was a fine example -"

"Now you know she was not the saint you have her to be," Judah said. "She even acknowledged she wasn't an angel. The main point of that marriage was a church merger. It was just luck that they liked each other and even luckier for you Josiah was ready to settle down after Daddy talked to us."

"At least Josiah was smart enough to not be caught in a crackhouse," Lavinia whispered. "You both are lucky I am a praying mother. Y'all would've not made it to adulthood if I wasn't on my knees every night."

"You may have prayed but you were not there during my withdrawals and helping me recover," Judah pointed out. "You were on your knees but Daddy was on the streets looking, sitting us down with ultimatums and trying to get us to explain the root of problems. And you keep throwing that part of my life in my face as if I am not capable of change after all these years. You did not hold my hand, wipe my face, stay awake to watch me sleep, forgive me for lashing out or walk in offices begging people to give me another chance."

"No Judah," Lavinia agreed. "I couldn't do that when I had over a thousand people relying on me to lead a service, handle business, counsel and run an international ministry. I had to be firm and give you tough love."

"Mama, I didn't need tough love, I needed help just like the other night, you saw what you wanted to see and you blamed her," Judah sighed. "I told you I think I had a problem. You told me to pray. I told Derika and she said we would get through it and let's get a professional team in. When me and Josiah came to you as children, you led us in prayer and - "

"Judah I do not have time to go dig up the past!" Lavinia said firmly. "This is about the future. You take the position."

"Pastor Jones thinks -" he began

"Paul don't think for you, I do," Lavinia said.

"He's on my advisory team as is Derika and we will discuss it," Judah picked up his file and went back to work. "You can shut the door when you leave."

"I'll send out the invitations next week," Lavinia said. "Only one hundred people. And none of your industry friends. This ain't no red carpet, it's the streets paved with gold."

CHAPTER 15

Between Derika being annoyed with him and Lavinia making demands of him on top of the pressures of running the church, Judah was feeling overwhelmed. He went by Josiah and Rachel's and sat in the basement where he and Josiah used to chat and play video games or watch movies, wishing for them. Rachel and Derika would be upstairs giggling and JJ would eventually stroll down saying they were making too much noise and sit with his father and uncle in the man cave. Maybe he and Derika should have moved in there or gotten another house but there was Darold. Judah felt he just needed to sit with Darold for a moment and hope some of his wisdom would impart.

"Hey Barbara," Judah said, knocking on the door as he walked in the bedroom his father was staying in.

Lavinia insisted he be placed outside of their bedroom because she didn't want her place of rest to be a hospital room and have people in and out. Judah hired a caregiver for his father who practically lived in the room to ensure she kept constant watch over Darold.

"Judah!" Barbara smiled. "Wasn't expecting you home so soon. Darold… you going to wake up and talk to Judah? Come now. Open your eyes again."

"He opened his eyes again?" Judah asked.

"Yes," she smiled. "Today when the children were getting into some argument he opened his eyes. They're lucky he didn't find the words to say what he wanted to say. But one of these days it will all make sense again. I wish you were here earlier to see his progress. And I put on your music too. He smiled. Even in this state he is proud of you."

"Has my mother been to see him?" held Darold's hand.

"Your wife came by this afternoon," Barbara said. "Told him she wished he was able to help her talk sense into you. She made him some soup and said maybe he'll smell it and wake up. Your wife asks daily how he's doing. Oh, and your daughter let him hear the song she sang at church. That little girl is so precious!"

"And my mother?" Judah asked again.

"She hasn't been this week," Barbara said.

"He is at home," Judah sighed. "She should be in here daily. Why don't you take a few hours to yourself? I'll keep an eye on him."

"Are you sure?" Barbara asked.

"I'm sure," Judah said. "I'll also send you a little gift on the app. And please accept it. You have been a tremendous help."

Barbara smiled and nodded.

"Darold… Judah is here now so I am going to go have dinner with my sister," she said. "Tell him what we talked about today, why don't you? What's that? Yes… I think he should read some more from the book of Psalms to you too."

"I appreciate you Barbara," Judah said as she gave him a hug.

"You continue to do what you do," Barbara said. "You are a wonderful son."

As soon as she left, Judah looked for his father's bible on the nightstand and didn't see it. He opened the drawer and found another bible. He also found a pen he recognized. He took them and sat in the chair facing Darold.

"Mama is going to cause a big awful situation," Judah said aloud. "All this stuff… you never trained me to do it because you knew Josiah would be the one to do it. I used to think he was lucky but this is more work than I thought it would be. I don't know how you could do this for so long."

Judah opened the bible and recognized it as Josiah's from when they were younger. He flipped through the pages and noticed notes and photos as bookmarks. He took a deep breath when he saw a photo of Rachel from middle school, then one of her when she was in high school and another with the three of them with other children when they were much younger. Judah noticed Rachel and Josiah were standing next to each other and Josiah was frozen in time looking at her. Judah chuckled when he saw a note written by Josiah asking Rachel to circle yes or no if she was going to be his girlfriend. She had written at the bottom, "if you want me to be your girlfriend you wouldn't ask me with a stupid paper so try harder". He found invites to parties, ordination ceremonies, ticket stubs and tucked away near the end of Genesis, he found another photo and folded paper and a page that had the names Ephraim and Manasseh highlighted. He recognized the paper before he opened it as lyrics to a song Josiah had written for him. His eyes filled with tears as he recalled them coming up with it and singing. Darold used to tell people they were his Moses and Aaron, ready to have each other's back but he prayed they would be blessed like the sons of Joseph who received the inheritance of Israel.

Tears flowed as Judah realized just how much he wanted one more chance to speak to Josiah. One more chance to hold him. He took the cover off the pen and put it to his nose. For a split second, he thought of what Derika would say if she knew he had hidden what he hid in the fake pen. But the part that needed a distraction from the hurt spoke louder and he inhaled. He groaned for a moment and shook his head immediately feeling it burn his nose for a moment. He took a deep breath and looked out the window.

"That ain't no help to you, boy," Judah imagined Josiah scolding him. "Put away childish things Judah."

"One pain numbs another," Judah replied. "It's the only way I know how."

"Oh yeah of little faith," he thought Darold would've said.

"Daddy, I'm trying, but this is Josiah's birthright, not mine," Judah sighed opening another fake pen.

"Don't you do it…" Darold's voice was louder.

Judah looked at his father. To his surprise, Darold was watching him.

"No temptation has seized you except what is common to man," Darold quoted scripture in a weak voice. "When you are tempted, he will provide a way for you to overcome it."

"Almost," Judah wiped his tears and went to Darold's bedside. "Almost got it right. I prayed for you to wake up."

"I heard you," Darold said. "I told you, you a prayer warrior."

"You just going to have a whole miracle recovery and start talking huh?" Judah laughed. "This must be why Barbara was trying to get me in here. She didn't want to tell me so I could see for myself."

"Jo said he's with his family and you need to be with yours," Darold said.

"After what we been through I don't know if I have a family," Judah sighed.

"She said you keep pushing her away," Darold said. "Dee sends me food. She is a forgiving woman. Don't lose her. Once you lose them you lost."

"Leave it to you to come back from the dead full conversation," Judah laughed. "You want me to tell Mama to come?"

"No," Darold said. "Barbara said to trust you, no one else. She told me to show you because you need faith."

"Well, I won't tell nobody else," Judah promised. "I love you, Daddy. I been wanting to say that to you."

"I love you, son," Darold said. "I'm finna rest now."

Judah nodded as tears of joy streamed down his face. Those words in that moment meant more to him than he ever knew they could. Barbara walked back in at that exact moment and quickly shut the door.

"I forgot my purse," she said.

"You didn't tell me," Judah said.

"Baby, he wanted to learn how to speak again first and then talk to you," she rubbed Judah's back. "Regular chatterbox he's been for about five weeks now. Comes and goes in spurts but now he's retaining memory. Then he just drifts off to sleep. Spend more time with him. He'll remember."

As Judah spent more time with Darold in private, he began to cope. He was able to handle his sermons better, counsel better and have something to look forward to. At Barbara's suggestion of dating to rekindle his marriage, he even found time to invite Derika to a lovely date at the aquarium, dinner and later a hotel suite.

"Are you still upset?" Judah asked her as she looked out the window.

"Of course, I am," she said. "But thank you for a wonderful evening. At least you put thought into it. I just want to lay down now."

She took off her dress and got under the covers. She immediately went on her phone to read through emails.

"You not going to watch tv?" she asked.

Judah hung his clothes over a chair and got into bed with her.

"Derika, I planned tonight for us to get out the house and try to reconnect," Judah reminded her.

"It was nice," she continued scrolling. "I appreciate the effort but I don't want to talk."

"Fine," Judah reached over and took her phone.

"What the hell?" she asked. "Give it back."

He tossed it to the chair and took her in his arms.

"Derika I'm trying to mend this," he begged. "Please talk to me."

"Judah... I have nothing to say," she sighed.

"We don't have to speak," he kissed her. "I would like for us to do this. Just us without all the extra."

She chuckled nervously realizing that she didn't remember the last time they did it without the extra.

"Fine," she said, turning her back to him.

"No," he insisted. "Come here. I need to see your face."

He kissed her, gently at first to break the ice but more passionately within the moment. She was taken off guard.

"The light..." she told him.

"Leave it on," he said.

"What the hell has gotten into you?" she asked.

"Maybe we do better with a bit of hell instead of heaven," he shrugged. "Just go with it."

"I need to get in the mood," she told him.

"Fine," he reached for his phone and put on music.

"Judah, there is no way we are doing this to your music," she laughed. "Turn that off!"

He turned off the phone and started singing to her.

"Judah, I don't know who the hell told you that it was cute but it wasn't me," she said.

"Every lover I have had loved me singing to them," he said.

"I have seen some of your so-called lovers who were impressed with things like electricity," she raised an eye. "I was the upgrade you needed."

"As long as you know," he kissed her again, this time she was far more receptive.

It felt different. It felt deeper. It felt far more connected. He explored every inch of her. For a brief second she wondered where he may have learned some things but the ecstasy that engulfed her made her forget what she was thinking. Their hands interlocked and they discovered a rhythm they hadn't played in years. She felt herself near her peak.

"Judah wait…" she tried catching her breath as she held onto his shoulders feeling the energy build between her legs. "Wait…"

"I can't, babe," he told her. "Look at me. Look at me, Dee."

Their eyes locked with each other and were suddenly synchronized. The trance continued as the adrenaline flowed. He found that part of her she thought he forgot about and at the same time, they released it, loudly.

"Are you crying?" Judah asked her.

"No," she smiled as she touched his tears. "You are."

"Wow," he chuckled, touching her tears.

"Wow," she repeated, kissing him, clearing all thoughts of Cameron from her mind.

He laid on his back and she instinctively rested her head on his chest and her leg over his. In each other's arms, they fell asleep knowing that they were at a new place with each other and it was a place that they needed to be. They knew that they would be in it against all odds, together.

CHAPTER 16

Derika hated the board meetings with the elders and she especially hated meeting on Sundays before service. They were not all old, but they were so caught up in their ways keeping the church on track that they did not seem to come down from their high horse. They dictated just as much as Lavinia did and now here they were signing documents as the church officially transferred to Judah. Today's meeting was not boring Derika as much as it usually did, especially since she was still on a high from her evening of reconciliation with Judah. She smiled to herself replaying the moment in her head.

"You must be proud Mother Waters," one of them remarked to Lavinia. "Your grandfather, father, husband and now both your sons have led Greater Gates."

"Mother?" Lavinia repeated.

"Well now that it will be official, Derika will be referred to as First Lady and you as Mother Waters," Paul told her as Derika smirked.

Lavinia chuckled as she reached into her pocketbook.

"Derika won't be here very long, Pastor Jones," she told him. "She's here for today but she's going to California tonight."

"No, I'm not," Derika said. "Lavinia… not today please."

"Is there a problem?" one of the deacons asked.

"Just a little private something between her and I," Derika assured him. "Nothing to interrupt my husband's moment."

"Now in the bylaws, there is something about the spouse of ministry leaders being unfit to continue in service and that person having to either confess their sins before the church or walk," Lavinia spoke up loudly. "Derika do you have anything you wish to share with us?"

"Mama, what are you doing?" Judah asked.

"Having you and the church's best interests at heart," she said. "Now, Derika, again… do you have anything you feel will keep you from being an adequate wife to our newly appointed leader?"

"Lavinia, I am not entertaining you today," Derika turned her head. "This is Judah's moment and I am not going to let anyone put a damper on it, not even you. Be blessed."

Lavinia took the envelopes she got from her purse and walked over to Judah.

"See for yourself," Lavinia threw an envelope on the desk. "This woman does not mean you well at all. Open it."

Judah sighed and opened it, shocked to see photos fall out. He looked at the photos as the others in the room wondered what he was seeing.

"What is this?" he asked.

"I got tired of her so I had her followed and good thing too," Lavinia admitted.

The photographer was able to get photos of Derika and Pat together at dinner and then walking into a car together. There was another shot of her walking with him into a hotel then walking out the next morning alone in the same dress.

"You sent her out there and sent Shay with her," Lavinia said. "I don't see no Shay in these pictures."

"This doesn't prove anything," Judah told his mother. "Mr. Smith and I arranged these meetings. He is unconventional and his time is scarce. Besides, we have some business together. Why would a teenager be at those meetings? Can we please get back to this? My apologies to everyone. Y'all know my mother is just a tiny bit overprotective after what happened."

Lavinia gave him another envelope.

"I guess this one is charity?" she said as he opened the envelope and the photos showed Cameron and Derika enjoying dinner then leaving in separate cars, then later arriving separately to his condo. The rest of the photos were explicitly detailed showing them on his sofa and kitchen counter. Judah put the photos face down.

"I'm not going to go through these," he said firmly.

"I have video too," Lavinia showed him her phone.

"That is an invasion of privacy!" Derika tried to charge at her but was held back.

"I told you from day one, I didn't want that whore of Babylon getting her claws in you and here she is, done sought out everything to destroy in her path!" Lavinia said sternly to Judah before turning to the board. "As board members, as elders, I do believe we have a right to advise Bishop Judah to divorce this woman because the bible did give adultery as the reason for leaving. The last thing we need is for her to bring this ministry down."

"Bishop, I'm inclined to agree with your mother," one of the pastors spoke up. "It's already been an adjustment with your celebrity status and now the tabloids and blogs are talking and we are not used to all of this."

"But the bible also encourages forgiveness, Mother Waters," Nick chimed in. "Maybe we ought to give him a moment and decide while we state no comment as these things come up."

"Or maybe she can have some dignity and walk before she is thrown out," Lavinia shrugged. "She is not worthy to cross the threshold into the sanctuary. Keep Fiona from her before she ends up destroying your house too."

"Judah..." Derika began.

"Oh no!" Lavinia pointed a finger at Derika. "You are to go out there and announce your divorce and you are going to explain why."

"Mama, this is something we have to discuss in private," Judah told her. "Let me just go out there and continue the sermon planned for today, then we can come back to this later."

"What else is there to discuss?" Lavinia asked. "Now, Judah I didn't want to do this but she left me no choice."

"First Lady, maybe we should wait to do things in private instead of airing out family matters," Paul said quietly.

"Now Pastor Jones, I don't know what kind of counseling you are giving them but you need to know when God is trying to pull something apart," Lavina pointed at Paul. "You should have told him to put her out."

Lavinia opened the envelope herself and gave it to Judah.

"After these photos, I said to myself, this heifer is too cunning and I gave the children a DNA test," Lavinia went through the papers. "You came through me so my grandchildren should have my DNA."

"Don't you dare bring my children into this," Derika warned.

"Lavinia, I am not going to sit here for this family strife," one of the deacons began to get up.

"Shut up!" Lavinia told him before walking to Derika. "You have nothing else to say all of a sudden, missy? Explain to me why that boy of yours carries Judah's name but doesn't even have his blood."

Gasps were heard as eyes went to Derika. Tears began falling down her face as she saw Judah read through the findings then turn the paper over.

"You are a wicked old woman..." Derika lowered her eyes as one of the men loosened her. "You just don't stop until someone is hurt do you?"

"It's a little too late for tears," Lavinia said. "Deaconess Roberts, isn't your son a divorce attorney? How soon can he have papers drawn up?"

"I'm done," Derika said, getting her handbag and walking out.

"You been done," Lavinia smiled, making the mistake of turning her back to Derika.

As Derika walked past Lavinia, she grabbed her by her hat and attacked. She managed to get in one punch before she was restrained, still with Lavinia's hair in her grasp.

"She ain't worth it, baby girl," Paul whispered to Derika. "No matter what no one says, this is between you and Judah. Now let her go."

Derika let Lavinia go and turned away from her.

"For now, I think this needs to remain in here until we decide what we will do," Paul advised everyone as he comforted Derika.

Some of the board members nodded in agreement while others shook their heads.

"Everyone… I thank you for your attendance and discretion, but I think this meeting needs to be adjourned," Judah said, turning his chair to look out the window. "We will go on as planned today but will have a meeting this afternoon. Derika… I need you to stay behind please."

Derika wiped her eyes quickly as Paul gave her a gentle pat, whispering to her that he would be right outside the door if she needed him.

"That was not the time nor place," Paul told Lavina as she walked out.

"It was going to be here amongst the twelve or out there," Lavinia chuckled. "I should have done that years ago."

"Pastor Jones and Melissa…" Judah called before he and Derika went through a door to his personal office. "Please wait at Melissa's desk. And Paul, I need you to make the phone call."

"Yes, Bishop," Melissa nodded as they stepped out and closed the door behind them.

Derika approached Judah with her lips trembling. She looked for an acknowledgment from him.

"Please…" she begged him to speak. "That wasn't even recent. I mean… it was but… Judah you know -"

"Sit," he pointed to the chair nearest to him.

They looked at each other for a moment then sat facing each other. They had been there before, calm and collective, honest and upfront. Their confessions were always something they shared together and moved on from.

"Did you have a relationship with Cameron?" Judah asked.

"It wasn't …" Derika tried to think before speaking. "I don't want to be with him but yes, I did sleep with him."

"Once?" Judah asked to which she nodded. "Twice?"

"Yes…" she replied

"Three times?" he continued.

Derika nodded.

"At least ten times?" he asked.

Derika looked down.

"Derika you're going to look at me and respond," he told her. "Look at me and tell me how long this has been happening!"

"It was nothing!" she insisted.

"How long?" he asked.

Derika blurted out everything in what seemed like an eternal confession. Judah turned away when she admitted it had gone on for about two years. She saw the hurt in his face when he learned of the time.

"Once is an accident, three times could be confusion, ten times is a whole relationship," Judah leaned forward. "All eyes on us and you get caught? How stupid could you be? You know my mother had it out for you. You know JJ is always on his phone looking up stories and stuff and you do this so he can read about it? Right before I get the highest title in this church and the overseer is about to declare it, you do this."

"I tried telling you!" she began crying.

"Everyone now knows Cameron Diggs paid the church a million dollars to fuck the bishop's wife," he shook his head. "No matter how good his intention was, how you tried to commemorate Rachel, you ruined it with this affair. They doubted me but my legacy was to bring this church from its darkest hour. Your legacy is going to be the church's most expensive piece of ass. I am so damn disappointed in you I don't even know what to say right now."

Derika began sobbing. This level of his anger was new to her.

"I can handle a conversation with you," Judah composed himself. "We always get through this in private and confront everything. But public shame? Do you have any idea how humiliating that was for me to sit through as she pulled up your files? Do you have any idea, Derika? You disgraced us and worse, this whole ministry. I don't even want to get started on JJ! I don't want to see you right now."

"I'm sorry," she fell at his knees sobbing. "I didn't think but I swear I didn't mean to."

"After everything, you do this?" he shook his head as she held his legs.

"Judah, please I'll do anything!" she pleaded.

"Anything huh?" he shook his head. "What would you do if I took Maya and me and my mother raised her?"

"I am begging you Judah, do not take away my child!" Derika cried uncontrollably. "Do not force me to live without them. I can't! Anything you want me to do I'll do! Just do not take them."

Judah didn't have the heart to separate the children or keep her away from them but he wanted to hurt as much as she made him hurt. He was disgusted at the thought of her and Cameron but angrier with her pulling the mask off of what people assumed to be a great marriage.

"Answer me this," Judah looked at her. "Did you suck his dick?"

"What?" she asked, confused.

"Did you suck Cameron Diggs' dick?" he asked. "Don't lie to me Derika."

She closed her eyes and nodded quickly, almost anticipating his hands around her neck strangling her. He'd never done it in malice but she felt it would be justified.

"Show me," he said.

"What?" she asked, shocked by his request.

"Now you don't remember what you did?" he asked, unbuckling his belt. "Show me what you did to him."

"Here?" Derika asked.

"I don't have all day Derika…" Judah said.

"I don't even remember," she lied.

"Oh you don't?" Judah asked. "I can't with you right now. Obviously, your mind is there, not here."

"Okay…" Derika said quickly, adjusting herself to take him.

After a few minutes Judah stopped her.

"I'm not done," she said, noticing he wasn't aroused.

"I am though…" he said.

"No…" Derika pleaded. "Let me try again. I can do better. See."

"How you think I feel knowing you had him up in every part of you?" Judah asked. "Derika I can't deal with that."

"Not every part of me, Judah," Derika assured him. "I promise you. I would never do with anyone what I do with you."

She stood and kissed him. He looked at the envelopes and photos on his desk and thought of her submitting to another man. He was already annoyed that Paul had confiscated his choice for euphoria and he needed to get in a mood to deal with everything.

"Turn around," he told her.

"What?" she said.

"Turn around and fix yourself," he directed her.

Derika complied knowing that if he was at least willing to touch her, she stood a chance at redemption. She reached under her dress and pulled down her underwear, then put her hands on the desk. She felt him raise her dress and push his way into her. She tried not to enjoy it but her body betrayed her and signaled to him that she did. Judah stepped back for a moment, now naturally lubricated by her, he repositioned himself higher and entered her another way.

"Did he do this?" he asked her as his pace increased.

"No…" she panted. "I would never."

"Did you use something?" he asked her.

"I would never expose us like that," she said between breaths. "You know I love only you."

He felt himself aroused by her words but didn't want her to know. Now his body betrayed him as he lost control and ejaculated. They stopped for a moment, bodies still connected but minds wondering what was to come next. She got a napkin and cleaned herself quickly then made herself appropriate.

"Do you want to talk some more?" she asked him.

"I want to look over the notes Paul gave me," he said sitting. "You can leave through the office door instead of going through the boardroom."

Derika opened the door and Paul and Melissa stood up quickly. She turned to walk off.

"Derika…" Paul gently touched her arm. "Please step back inside."

"It's best if I leave," she said.

"Come now," Paul said, leading her back in. "Melissa, give us a few minutes."

Paul and Derika walked back in together just as Judah tried to hide a small packet.

"This is why you can't leave right now," Paul told her. "Judah, you have come too far to fall back, son. Do not do it."

"Pastor Paul -" Judah started to say.

"All of your help cometh from God," Paul said. "He is your high not that, son. You are better than this. I am not letting you get any titles in here with this in your system."

Judah reluctantly surrendered the bag.

"Now I said I was going to help you," Paul handed him some papers. "These are some notes I made and I already emailed it. And you Derika, you are going to have to humble yourself and let him take the lead. Yes, there is gossip but mark my word there are more people who would rather stay if you show how forgiving you are to her. So do not punish her right now, Judah. Win this congregation. Believe that he can turn it in your favor."

"I can't go out there," Derika said.

"You are going to and you're going to do it right and you Bishop are going to get it together," Paul told them. "Accept each other and yourselves. Forgiving, maturing and leading by example. I don't care about Lavinia or y'all, but God is the ultimate judge and y'all will not disrespect he who is the author and finisher of all things. You've had sickness and health, now deal with better or worse. Get through the next few hours and move on."

CHAPTER 17

"You have no right to sit up here in this sacred space," Lavinia said as Derika sat in the seat next to Judah's.

"Lavinia, we agreed to get through today and make decisions in the next few weeks," Paul told her as he took his seat. "We don't need any humiliation or nothing. Derika is Bishop's wife and this is where she will be seated today."

"Paul, do not make me force my hand," Lavinia warned. "Get her out of this church. I will protect Greater Gates at all costs."

Derika drowned out Lavinia as she listened to the choir. She and Judah agreed to get through the day and then have a heavy counseling session with Paul. He planned on advising them to take some time to work harder with each other, and to prove to the board that they were capable, at least until a suitable replacement was made.

"First Lady Derika Waters will now bring a few brief remarks," Derika heard the moderator call her name. "First Lady?"

She and Lavinia quickly looked at Paul. He mouthed the word 'go' to Derika and she got up just as Judah took his seat. He clasped his hands together as the unsuspecting church applauded.

"It's a great day at Greater Gates, amen?" she said nervously into the mic. "This past year has been… a big change for all of us but I am truly proud of what you all have accomplished as a congregation. Without that support, I don't think Judah would have been able to do it. As for my role here today, it's to introduce my husband to you as he makes this next step in his journey. Judah… Bishop Waters is the type of person who is not afraid of a challenge and who values legacy. This church is his home and -"

A collective gasp was heard. Derika looked up and saw the congregation in shock, some checking their phones while others looked behind her.

"Take that down!" she heard Paul say. "Who is in the media room?"

Derika looked at Lavinia who smirked back at her and then looked up to the main monitor. There was a video clip of Derika with Cameron, his back to the camera so people were not sure who it was but her face was clearly visible, eyes closed, mouth slightly opened and clearly enjoying the moment. She realized a mass text had been sent out to the congregation's phone. The voices got louder and people expressed their disgust with her. Derika wanted so badly to escape. She turned and bumped into Judah.

"Fuck this church," Judah muttered as he made his way to the pulpit in the midst of the commotion.

The video was already on the main monitors and obviously shared on the phones.

"Whoever is in the media room, shut this shit down now!" Judah shouted into the microphone. "And cut the livestream. Everyone calm down."

"Well I came to worship not see you and your wife's sex tape!" a deaconess stood.

"Girl, that was her but it wasn't him," another woman said.

"Sin in the camp!" someone else shouted. "Sin is in the camp!"

"Sin in the camp and you're in the camp so that means you ain't nothing but another sinner in the camp!" someone else shouted back.

"Well I'm leaving this hell hole!" another person called. "I am not going to be covered by a church that has all this foolishness at the head. Y'all all going to hell. My soul ain't joining a one of you! That's what happens when you give the church to a musician."

Judah's palms were sweaty as he held onto the pulpit amid the shouting in Greater Gates Church. He felt his chest tightening and his collar choking him. He looked at the photos of the church's bishops on the wall and stared for a moment at the photo of his brother, Josiah. So much had changed within a year. So much. He'd been given an assignment and failed it. Now his family and church was paying the price.

He felt a gentle hand cover his, and suddenly felt the courage to open his eyes again.

"Now, everybody is going to calm down and we are going to hear the truth," he found his voice.

"Oh, I don't have to stay here for this," someone else got up.

"Sit down and hush up!" Judah commanded. "Now all y'all just calm down. I didnt want to have to go here but enough is enough. Everyone in here has sin. And I am not going to let you all attack each other."

"We ain't attacking each other," a voice shouted at him. "We just want *that* woman gone! Cast her out!"

Judah looked at his wife Dericka as she gave his hand a squeeze.

"We stick together…" she said. "Whatever, you decide. I trust you to make the right decision even if that means parting."

The monitor went blank. Paul realized that Lavina had leaked the information after she saw Derika was not going to be forced out. It was her last card and he had to admit, it looked like the ace to finally win the game.

"Then Jesus stood up again and said to the woman, 'Where are your accusers who condemn you?'," Judah spoke, his voice seemingly bringing order to the crowd. "She said 'Lord, there are none left'. And he told her to go and sin no more. So you can do one of two things, Greater Gates. Hit forward or hit delete but whichever one of you is without sin, please cast the first stone."

Paul smiled as he saw the leader he knew was within Judah emerge. Though embarrassed, Derika felt a sense of comfort hearing Judah say what he did instead of condemning her.

"Great sermon Bishop but your wife is a ho'!" someone stood up. "And I'm not calling no ho' first lady!"

"Sit down and I'll explain," Judah said. "I'm not asking y'all to stay but I do ask that we have a heart to heart right now. I owe you that just as you have opened up to accepting and electing me to this position. And you all are right. Derika was never designed to be a First Lady of a church. She told y'all this from day one. And honestly, I never wanted to do anything more than sing and not just gospel music but I felt I had to stay in the box because of what you expected of me."

Several of the people who were on their way to walk stopped and sat back down to listen to Judah. It was as if he was addressing them as himself for the first time, unrehearsed.

"The truth is sin is sweet," he admitted. "Now, all this time you are blaming her for her transgressions, sins she does not deny, but you are not seeing the whole picture. Before our marriage vow, Derika and I made an agreement that we would protect each other against all costs. The thing is she is my best friend and she tells me I am hers. And just like the rest of y'all we have great days and we have mad days. This past year, we have had more mad days and bad days than we had in the ten years we have been together. And it's tiring."

"Amen Bishop!" someone shouted at him.

"Thank you brother, you over there sounding like you know about that couch life too," Judah joked, prompting a giggle and softening the mood. "We have had some dark days. Like some of you older ones know about my substance abuse and alcohol addiction. Even after one of my best friends was killed doing something because I needed that one last fix, I didn't quite let it go until my wife and brother stepped in. She helped me fight through it and Josiah, my brother who protected me then and watches over me now, it was Josiah who came and prayed and covered me and helped her when my own mother disowned me. And y'all can ask Pastor Jones about that part because he and my daddy saw the worst of it, searching the streets for me when I was lost."

Lavinia shook her head at Judah for painting her in a negative light while he uplifted Derika. The church was bending to side with Derika and that was not the plan.

"Are you going to tell them that this isn't the first time she has done what she did to you?" Lavinia asked. "She trapped him with another man's baby! She did that! Marriage by false pretenses. Is there a divorce lawyer in the house?"

"It was Josiah and Derika who taught me unconditional love and that love goes beyond blood or marriage," Judah spoke up over the confused voices. "You see my wife, in your eyes she has sinned, but in my eyes she has made the ultimate sacrifice of proving there is no greater love than laying her life down for a friend. No, our son is not my biological son but I was there through every scan, cut the umbilical cord, held him before my wife did, and if any of you have a problem with me giving my child my name and my heart, then you have an issue with Joseph taking Mary to be his wife and raising Jesus as his child."

The congregation cheered him. Lavinia stood up and clapped her hands sarcastically.

"You must be so proud of yourself, Delilah!" she told Derika. "Over a hundred years we put into this ministry and you single-handedly brought it down with your whoring ways. You need to leave and go and find the real father of that child and make him take care of this boy and change his name!"

"The same way you could accept Josiah and Rachel adopting a child, why can't you accept our son?" Derika asked.

"You used that boy to trap my child into marrying you," Lavinia told her. "Who is his real father?"

"I don't know!" Derika's eyes filled with tears. "I don't know."

"Typical," Lavinia scoffed.

"She doesn't know because she and I went somewhere together and I was high downstairs while she was being raped upstairs," Judah blurted out. "There. Now you know. End of the day, his name is Judah Waters, Jr and I am his father. Period. She didn't even know she was pregnant and then once she found out, she did not want to take the life of an unborn child and felt that no one would respect her. So I gave her her dignity to be able to hold her head high and said it was my child and he is. I also gave her my name as a way of protecting her because the truth is when people found out she was my wife all of a sudden it was a barrier they knew they would not be able to cross. So excuse me for giving my wife and my son a place of peace and the security they need to survive in this world."

"You are a good man Bishop!" someone called to him.

"You are an overcomer First Lady Derika!" Faith called out. "We support you!"

Derika felt a sense of relief now the world knew. She wiped the tears from her eyes as Judah put an arm around her.

"Shame on her to bring down her son's wife like that," someone whispered loud enough for Lavinia to hear.

"Lavinia, I think I am going to be fine with Judah remaining as is," one of the deacons sitting near Lavinia told her.

"You watch when you get home, missy!" Lavina warned Derika.

"My wife is an incredible mother and I will not have anyone bringing up our children unless they looking to get the side of God that sends floods and fire and brimstone," Judah warned.

"As you should!" Shay shouted. "Preach on preacher!"

Derika felt overwhelmed to finally hear him publicly stand up for her to Lavinia.

"Paul Jones, come on up here," Judah called Paul to him. "Now over the years, since I was a child, I have seen you dedicate yourself to this church and the congregation, to my family and to the faith."

Paul seemed puzzled as Judah walked him to the pulpit. Judah took a deep breath and spoke to the congregation.

"I have discussed this the national overseer right after you left the meeting before service and I will be stepping down effective immediately, and Pastor Paul Jones is your Interim Bishop and once a date is set, he will be ordained as leader of this church," he announced. "Deacon Nick Prescott, I have personally recommended you to the senior pastor position. I have also put forth five women for consideration of pastors, a first for this church. We are not discriminating gender but believing that we can all be used. Turns out, you can amend a few clauses when you have been Bishop for only ten minutes."

Confusion was heard amidst the applause as Paul and Judah embraced.

"Judah, now you stop this nonsense!" Lavinia spoke up. "Paul isn't even married and women are not designed to lead the church!"

"What does that have to do with it?" Judah asked. "This is not a monarchy, Mama. My heart is not in this. I can't go another Sunday like this. Bishop Jones is best and Senior Pastor Prescott is more than capable. And women will be allowed to step up if that is their call."

"Look what you caused you vicious little Delilah!" Lavinia growled as she approached Derika. "Judah, she has taken your strength and birthright and ruined you and this church!"

"Lavinia I have had just about enough of you!" Derika shot back. "You can't handle knowing you are not the only woman in his life. You can't handle that you couldn't break him to bend to you."

"Enough!" Judah said. "You are so fixated on what she did wrong, it never occurred to you that she was my escape from your expectations. You never saw how she protected me."

"Brothers and sisters, we are going to adjourn service a bit early today but please stop for refreshments," Lavinia smiled as she took a mic.

"You can't even let him leave on his terms can you?" Derika hissed at Lavinia.

"Girl, if you don't back it up you will meet your maker and I know he will welcome you into the lake of fire that you belong in!" Lavinia warned. "I don't understand why he kept you after that mess. What can you possibly give him?"

"You really want to know?" Judah asked facing her. "Because I am a bit sick and tired of all this for all these years. She gives me the mask I need to be myself. I hid behind my wife because I knew you would never accept a gay son."

"Judah!" Derika covered his mic.

Alphonso smiled proudly, hearing Judah say what he knew to be true for years, while others gasped in disbelief.

"No..." Judah moved Derika's hand to uncover the mic. "These people have trusted me and I am not going to betray them. I don't care if this ends my career, my life... I am a gay man... There. I said it publicly."

Shock waves swept the congregation. Lavinia looked at him stunned, her eyes filling with tears.

"You know what a beard is?" Judah asked her. "It covers your true face and in the gay community, it's a term used to hide one's true identity by having someone pretend to be your love interest and act as if you straight. I am so sick of the hypocrisy of it all. People know the truth but don't speak it. The church has for years earned off the backs of people who had to hide."

"Don't you dare!" Lavinia closed her eyes in disgust. "After all we put into this, you out here confessing to be a sodomite? God makes gladiators and Satan makes sissies!"

"Woman behold thy son," Judah opened his arms to her. "That's another reason I knew JJ wasn't my child because at that point in time, I had never even been with a woman. You think I married her to hurt you but I married her to please you."

"You knew?" Lavinia asked Derika. "You turned my son gay?"

"Oh sis, he been gay!" Alphonso waved a hand at her. "He just not a flamboyant bottom. He's the blend in on the down-low power bottom. If anything, she likely turned him bi which is how you became a grandmother."

"And I've had just enough of you old rainbow faggot!" Lavinia screamed at Alphonso. "You ain't nothing but a circus and I don't know why my husband let you stay in this church so long knowing damn well what you are!"

"God loves me, honey," Alphonso told her. "It's you who has a hate for gays. The very thing you hate ends up on your doorstep. That's why God placed a fish in your womb to swim around for nine months like Jonah and the whale - no disrespect to you Judah but your mama done crossed the line. But yes girl, last time your son found freedom in a vagina it was on his way coming out of you!"

"That's outright hate speech and we are not tolerating that in here Lavinia," Paul told her. "You can leave now and apologize later. I will not have you speaking to anyone like that. And Alphonso, this is not a roast session."

"My apologies Bishop Jones," Alphonso nodded respectfully.

"Oh hush!" Lavinia told Alphonso before turning to Derika. "Well... I suppose I ought to thank you for giving me a granddaughter. Next time don't put yourself in a position to be raped especially with the clothes you wear."

Lavinia began walking off then shook her head as she looked at Judah and without warning, ripped the collar off his neck.

"As for you, don't you ever walk through these hallowed halls again," she told him. "With the death of Josiah, I am now a childless mother."

"Is he not made in God's image and likeness?" Derika asked Lavinia.

"God wasn't no sissy!" Lavinia said before being led away. "Bishop Jones, control your congregation."

Judah and Derika held hands as they walked off the stage and headed towards the front door. The only thing he wanted was to hold his children, tell his father goodbye and retreat.

"Take me as I am Lord, when the world sees my wrong," Shay began singing the song that set the pace for Judah's career. "I've hidden behind this mask Lord, for far too long. They may hate the sinner, you may hate the sin. But you love me unconditionally, and you see my truth within."

Judah looked over and smiled at her.

"Judah... the Lord has a way of using people, even in their imperfect state, to do his will," Paul said, holding out a mic. "If he can use a donkey to see an angel, or a burning bush to speak to a murderer on the run, surely he has work for you."

"Use him Lord!" someone shouted prompting others to stand and cheer him on.

"You know you want to," Derika whispered, hugging him. "Just don't strain your voice. And remember... we are in this together."

"Bet," he smiled, giving her a quick kiss. "Together."

Judah took off the robe as he walked back up to take the mic feeling more like himself in his own clothes.

"My brother Josiah… when I told him who I thought I was, he wrote that song for me," Judah said, taking the mic. "I haven't sang that in years."

"Well you going to sing it today, brother!" Alphonso said, directing the choir to stand. "We're following you."

For the first time while singing the song, tears fell down Judah's face as he understood the sincerity and confession written for his personal conversation. He also mourned Josiah as he thought of what could have been had he not died. It was time to change and everything was going to be just fine.

CHAPTER 18

Judah and Derika walked into the house chatting, with a sense of joy in their voices after being invited to Sunday dinner with the Prescotts and a few others. Fiona and Nick let everyone know that they are not to judge but to leave it to the Lord and to continue to be the village they need in whatever decision is made. It was good knowing that some of the church members were truly friends and Derika was looking forward to keeping the Prescotts in their circle, especially with the children getting on as well as they did.

As Judah closed the door, Derika stopped in her tracks when she saw Lavinia still dressed in her church clothes sitting in her armchair in the parlor. Derika instinctively pulled her children closer to her as Judah stepped in front of them.

"You two are something else," Lavinia said without looking at them. "Come here Maya...JJ. Let me look at you."

The children looked up at their mother. Everyone at dinner earlier agreed, especially for JJ's sake, not to mention what happened and they had no idea of what went on while they were in the children's ministry. Derika hesitated but loosened them and walked them over to Lavinia.

"You look so much like me at your age," Lavinia touched Maya's hair. "Smart like me too. I used to like singing like you too but now, I don't have time to sing these days."

"God loves it when you sing praises to him," Maya told her, like her brother, oblivious to what transpired earlier.

"He does!" Lavinia nodded.

"Mommy says he understands you even if you forget the words," she continued. "God knows your heart and if you need him just ask him for help. He doesn't always say yes, but he's not a genie granting wishes. He does what's best in his time, not ours. So if you have a problem ask God to fix it. Mommy says he understands even if we don't."

"Mommy is a very wise woman," Lavinia said. "A much wiser woman than I thought she was. You listen to her and be a good girl. My prayers just not what they used to be."

"You praying but you don't have faith," Maya shrugged. "You need some annointing and some oil. Put some honda in your shonda."

"Oh my Maya!" Lavinia hugged her again.

"You good Grandma?" JJ asked, noticing her eyes were sorrowful. "Mom said you weren't feeling good and you came home early when we went to the Prescotts."

"I had a headache," Lavinia turned to him, her eyes filling with tears as she touched his face. "I want you to know that I love you JJ and I know you are going to be just fine."

"What's wrong Grandma?" JJ asked.

Judah turned to look away for a second and noticed a photo of him and Josiah with JJ as a toddler. That was the day they found out both Rachel and Derika were expecting.

"She's almost four months," Josiah had revealed. "This is the longest she's made it. We make it a few more weeks we can tell people. If she doesn't make it, I don't want to do it again. It's stressful and I cant take her hurting anymore. I don't even want to go in that nursery again and that's where she spends all her time."

"Well I pray everything goes well," Judah smiled. "You'd be amazing parents."

"You are an amazing parent," Josiah looked at JJ sleeping on Judah. "That child is blessed to have you. I admit I was a bit skeptical when you said you were going to marry her but yall are rock solid. I just wish you had the full experience of a marriage, you know."

"So… she's pregnant too," Judah told Josiah. "Literally just found out today."

"Who?" Josiah asked. "Derika? For who?"

"What do you mean for who?" Judah laughed. "We are married ain't we?"

"You and her… so it's a consummated marriage?" Josiah's eyes widened. "Well damn. Welcome to the team. Hell… more like welcome to the league."

"Boy hush up," Judah told him jokingly.

"Are you sure it's your baby?" Josiah asked. "I mean you know how women work, right? It's been years since I tried to tell you so you sure?"

"Of course it's mine," Judah replied. "She hadn't done anything since the incident and we were just drinking and things happened and then it happened again and then it happened sober and then it kept happening and it's not that bad. It's actually not bad at all."

"And you're comfortable with meeting all her needs but yours not being met?" Josiah asked. "Because that can be a problem. She knows your preference and she's missing something that your preference comes with."

"She met my needs, believe that," Judah said quietly. "We watched some stuff and brought some stuff and tried some stuff. She's pretty open to whatever and I mean, to whatever. She has an alpha side. She actually enjoys giving it as much as I enjoy receiving it."

Josiah put his hands up as he laughed.

"Receiving?" he laughed. "TMI bro. I do not need to get your specifics on y'all little freaky deaky and if my wife tries to talk me into any mess I'm blaming y'all."

"I just didn't know women were so… so… you know?" Judah tried to explain.

"Wait a minute," Josiah leaned in. "Is this the first time you've been with a woman? Like ever? All those girls you dated talking about you being such a gentleman you never?"

"Nah never," he admitted.

"Kinda sweet," Josiah smiled. "You both get to have this second virginity with each other. It's a first for you and for her."

"What's sweet is we get to be first-time fathers together," Judah looked at his brother.

"Nah… you're already a parent and a protector to this little man," Josiah rubbed JJ's head. "You don't need to share blood to be a parent. Besides, we know that blood doesn't make you a good parent. The good thing is he looks just like his mom's side so I doubt anyone is ever going to question it. But I am happy for you."

"I am happy for you," Judah said.

They heard Derika scream excitedly then run out to where they were sitting.

"You're going to wake him," Judah warned her as JJ stirred.

"So what!" she smiled as Rachel came out behind her and she hugged her. "JJ you're getting a cousin!"

"We're not saying anything yet," Rachel pulled up her sweater to show the small bump. "My mom knows but we want to make sure we are in the safe zone before we tell other people."

They all shared a few weeks later. Just after that, Rachel ended up with complications and miscarried the baby. While she was able to bounce back and helped Derika with Maya, Josiah was broken with another loss. He told Judah that even if Maya didn't come along, he was still fortunate with JJ and to continue to be an incredible father to both of them. Judah promised he would.

Judah shook his head and came back to the present. He looked at Lavina hugging JJ and realized that the secret they planned to keep from him was going to have to be told to him by them before someone else mentioned it.

"Derika please get him from her," Judah instructed.

"Come let's go upstairs and pack," Derika walked forward and reached for the children. "Tell Grandma goodnight."

"Raising children is hard work Derika," Lavinia looked at her. "I tried. But I ate sour grapes and my children's teeth were on edge. All these years you... Thank you... I think I see what you were trying to do. You should've told me."

"Lavinia I don't -" Derika began but was shocked when Lavinia stood up and hugged her.

Derika let go of the children and hugged her back. It was the first time she felt warmth in a hug from Lavinia. It was long overdue but there was finally a sense of peace between them.

"Dee..." Judah called to her. "It's late."

"Don't let them forget me," Lavinia said quietly as Derika let go.

Derika turned to lead the children upstairs as Lavinia watched them, sure it might be the last time she saw them. Judah began to follow them.

"Go talk to her," Derika whispered to him.

"I don't have time for that," Judah said. "We got to pack."

"JJ, take your sister upstairs and get changed," Derika instructed. "I'll be up there in a minute."

Judah looked at the wall as the children ran off shutting their doors behind them. He turned when he heard the front door open.

"Is this a good time?" Paul asked. "I wanted to come by earlier than later."

"This is the perfect time," Judah said. "Let me get you the keys to Josiah's house and please feel free to take whatever you need from my father's office. I'll be leaving a memo with the house staff so they know you can come and go."

"Just a moment please, Paul," Derika told him before turning her attention back to Judah. "Talk to her, Judah."

"After all she put you through, you want me to talk to her?" he shook his head. "All these years of trashing you, not giving you a chance, trying to break us up more than once. Disrespecting you in front of people… in front of our children?"

"She's your mother," Derika reminded him. "I would give anything if my mother were alive to speak to her."

"What kind of mother sends a private investigator after her daughter-in-law and leaks the findings like that?" asked Judah. "She forced me to tell the world something we agreed was going to stay buried in the past. It's just a matter of time before JJ finds out what she did. He's a child Derika… She made me out myself when that was no one's business but mine. My life and career is over. Fuck talking to her. She will never see the children again and she will never see me again. She said it herself. She is a childless mother."

Derika put her arms around him and he began to sob.

"You don't know what tomorrow holds, son," Paul stepped forward. "Now you said you want me as your spiritual advisor. I'm advising you to take this moment to speak to your mother. Cry it out if you need to but I think you need to put your cards on the table now and ask forgiveness later."

"Y'all made him a sissy, treating him all soft like that instead of making him man up," Lavinia sat back down. "Hiding behind Josiah, hiding behind Darold, hiding behind Derika, having them fight his battles. I should've known something was wrong when they were boys. Josiah was out slangin' dick, being reckless, risking putting our good name on a bastard.. This one was a dyslexic fool who couldn't read music and had to play by ear. Darold had an obligation to God first, family second."

Judah's chest rose and fell as Lavinia chastised him and brought up more of his flaws. A part of him that he had been suppressing for decades suddenly surfaced. He broke free from Derika, rushed across the room, pulled up another chair and sat in front of Lavinia and looked her in her eyes. She sat up straight, unintimidated by his need to speak.

"Hurry up and say it since you feel grown," Lavinia dared Judah.

"I have hated you since I was a child," he told her on the brink of tears. "You lifted up Josiah but put me down. You are going to listen to me. Josiah and I were messed up. We were messed up because we were molested by your brother every Sunday he offered to take us for ice cream. I told you I didn't like going with him and you forced me to go every time. And if you knew what Josiah did to protect me... He was the same age as my son is now. I can't imagine my children living in that fear but you knew. You knew."

Paul shook his head in disbelief as Derika seemed proud that Judah was speaking up. She knew that was the reason behind it all but let Judah deal with it in his way.

"And another thing, I'm not dyslexic," Judah continued. "I just couldn't concentrate reading a damn scripture when someone who was a pastor and a relative was doing that to us. And when Josiah told you what happened, you told him to hush up and you'd deal with it. All of a sudden, your brother is a pastor of another church. You had him at home for the holidays and we were supposed to smile like a happy family on Sunday. That's why I found comfort in music and a friend in alcohol and drugs. In order to tolerate that, I had to be high. Josiah was promiscuous because he felt that the more girls he was with then he would eventually forget it. He wasn't sowing oats. He was coping. Just like I was coping. A real mother would've reported it and gotten her children therapy."

"Judah, I do not have to sit here and listen to these lies," Lavina began to get up again. "I didn't molest you and I sure as hell didn't get you hooked on drugs. And if you were molested by a man why grow up to enjoy being a sodomite? You are weak! You knew how to go to God for yourself. I'm not listening to this mess."

"You sit and listen to me for a change!" Judah pushed her back in her seat.

"Have you lost your cotton-picking mind?!" she asked. "You tried to assault me?"

"Calm down, Judah," Paul warned him.

"Mama look at me," Judah got her attention. "Yes, I am married. Yes, I have children. But I am -"

"Don't you say it!" Lavinia covered her ears.

"I am a gay man," he told her. "I am a homosexual. Bisexual I suppose is more correct. I have an attraction for the person who my wife is, but not necessarily an attraction to women. I enjoy sleeping with men. Some of the men I introduced to you as friends were my lovers. Cody. Lewis. Marco…"

"You were married when Marco died," Lavinia shook her head.

"Yes," Derika said. "And it took him some time to get over that. That is the real reason he is committed to Shay. He promised Marco."

"Stop it!" Lavinia begged him. "That boy was a thug and you were… sissying each other? And had her comfort you? You tricked her, you sodomite! You brought men into your marriage?"

"And?" he shrugged. "As long as we know, we are good with it. My wife is allowed to sleep with other men under conditions we have agreed on. One of those conditions is that we sometimes do it together because a third is just our thing if we desire that. But we are committed to each other, no one else. Yeah. I was mad about Cameron but that was because he did not have my permission and she kept it from me. We have full disclosure with this and don't keep each other out of the loop."

Paul had taken out his handkerchief, wiped his face and took a seat by the time Judah stopped talking. He looked at Derika as she made her way to the liquor cart.

"Are you still up for being our counselor?" she asked him as Lavinia held her chest.

"I made a commitment," Paul chuckled. "Y'all two are about to give me a reason to change my insurance plan. I'm a need to put on the full armor if I am handling this."

"Brandy?" Derika offered as she poured a glass for herself.

"Scotch," he said.

They took seats and waited for Lavinia to recover from the state of shock she was in when she heard Judah put all the cards on the table.

"You are an adulterer and a sodomite!" Lavinia growled at Judah when she finally caught her breath. "I didn't raise y'all to be no faggots."

"That word is offensive," Judah told her.

"Would you prefer me to say ass digger?" she asked. "You've been over six feet tall since you were twelve. You're too damn big to be a sissy! Jesus, Jesus, Jesus, Jesus! And on top of that when you finally do have a woman willing to marry you after all that... that filth... you give your wife to other men? You give *yourself* to men? Both of you demons need to get up from under my roof."

"Out of respect to Derika, Judah, maybe you shouldn't reveal all your private life," Paul suggested.

"Derika doesn't care anymore," Derika said, pouring herself another glass. "She put my pictures out to every member with a phone. Derika is just glad that Judah is finally able to speak up for himself and tell her what he has been bottling up all these years. I'm proud of you, baby! Say what you have to say."

"You let him pimp you, you slut," Lavinia said. "I'm not listening to anything no more!"

Lavinia covered her ears.

"No, you're going to listen to everything," he moved her hands. "The only way I can be intimate with my wife is if she does to me what men have done to me. That is why we have dildos and strap-ons and other things for her to peg me with, and if she is in the mood for it, she allows me to perform anal sex on her. She enjoys it and I enjoy it and we have a dynamic that works for us because we still choose to be together. So those photos of Pat were not news to me. He's a straight guy who enjoys a discreet pegging now and again. Like it or not, this is who I am."

Lavinia slapped him across the face. He took a deep breath and looked away.

"There are some things a mother does not need to hear from her child!" Lavinia clenched her fist. "The last thing I needed to hear was that you enjoy being bent over and penetrated like the little bitch you are! I reject and rebuke you in the name of Jesus! I am not hearing no more!"

"What you should have been hearing you closed your ears to," Judah said. "Mama, I'm a man attracted to other men, and I am married to a woman who is okay with us on occasion having affairs with other men."

"And you just let him defile your marriage bed?" Lavina looked at Derika. "The one time you should put your foot down you don't! What kind of woman allows such entanglements in her marriage?"

"I'm standing by him," Derika said. "We actually love each other."

"Girl, ain't no woman is standing by a man who takes as much dick as she does," Lavinia shook her head. "Just leave. You leave and don't come back to church, to this city, and especially this house!"

"He doesn't have to leave," a voice startled them all.

They turned and saw Darold in a wheelchair being pushed by Barbara.

"I can not believe the words I heard come out of your mouth, Lavinia," Darold's voice, though weak, still had authority. "After all these years of lies you can't forgive him for choosing to live his life as he wants?"

"Darold you're awake," Lavinia walked over to him in disbelief.

"Roll me on over there," he instructed Barbara. "I've been awake. Woke. I'm woke like the kids say. And I'm woke to your ugly heart. What are you going to do when you stand before the throne to be judged? We've lost one son, a daughter and a granddaughter. Do not lose the only thing we have left."

"Some things cannot be forgiven," Lavinia told him.

"Like you not telling me why you got rid of your brother after he did what he did?" Darold asked. "All these years, you knew and never said anything. I would've never known unless Judah told me himself just recently. I wish he were alive so I could kill him dead for what he did to my boys. How many others did he touch? You never told me. God will deal with you. But my son and his family belong here."

"I live a righteous life," Lavinia pointed a finger at him. "I live a holy life. I raised my children as I raise the church and I will not allow them in our lives or the church until they get right."

"Judge not, that you be not judged," Darold quoted. "For with the judgment you pronounce you will be judged, and with the measure you use it will be measured to you."

"The adulterers and fornicators and harlots and men who lie with men shall be cast into the lake of fire…" Lavinia spoke as if she were on a pulpit. "Judah… I am done with you. Leave. And take Delilah on with you."

"All this time, I laid in that bed, thought I would never wake up," Darold looked at Paul. "I kept hearing what I heard that horrible day. Kept seeing it over and over saying when I opened my eyes, Josiah would be there waiting. Then I woke up and realized it was real. You don't know humility until your son dresses your wounds, changes your soiled clothes, bathes you, teaches you to talk again the way my Judah did. Those two children came in every day to ask

Barbara if I was up yet. This daughter I was blessed to gain came in every day with something for me to smell from the kitchen. Church folk came. Everyday after school, my grandson talked to me. Maya, she sang to me. I heard them but couldn't respond. You never came, Lavinia. I'm not putting him out. You leave."

"You can't make me leave," Lavinia laughed.

"I'm tired of you Lavinia," Darold shook his head. "I'm filing for divorce and I want you gone by the weekend."

"Now Darold, I know you don't expect this of me but she has nowhere to go," Derika spoke up. "Please reconsider. Everyone is just tense now but maybe by morning we'll be better?"

"Derika, you are a good woman," Darold extended a hand for her to hold. "The stone the builder rejected... You are too good to have taken this foolishness from her all this time. Lavinia, I want you to either apologize to Judah and Derika or leave. You don't have to accept him but you will love him unconditionally."

Lavinia looked at everyone in the room. She cleared her throat, smoothed her hair and went off to her bedroom.

"How long you been up?" Derika asked hugging Darold. "I missed your voice in here."

"We agreed he would keep it quiet," Judah told her. "The overseer knows and Paul knew. Next week, if Barbara says it's okay, we'll take him to church."

"For a little while," Barbara said.

"My brother, my friend," Paul smiled. "It's good to have you back."

"Bishop Jones..." he smiled. "Thank you."

CHAPTER 19

Judah closed his eyes and listened to the music through his headphones on nearly fully blast. It was the way to feel it properly. It took it all in. The beat, the instruments, the lyrics, the vocals. He smiled as the song ended. This was his element and he was happy to be back in it, churning out items in his home studio.

"Judah?" his producer Mac called his name. "You want me to run it again?"

Judah turned his chair to face the recording booth and looked at Shay.

"Yes?" she said nervously from the booth.

"I think we got it, baby girl," he smiled. "That track is officially done!"

"Aye!" Shay gave a little dance. "Now I can do my music video! I was thinking beach theme, me in a bikini -"

"You need to practice on singing this live before you worry about a video little girl," he laughed. "And you can keep the crop tops and bikini tops but you keep your unmentionables unmentioned."

"Alphonso is sending me a few wardrobe options and he also asked Asmera Jacobs-Powers to send a dress for the music video," Shay told him. "I'll be good for my shoot and the awards show appearance."

"Proud of you," he said. "You have a top one hundred single and now you have a complete album. But I don't care hw famous Xiamora is, Shay has rules to abide by in here."

"And I have a duet with you!" she gave him a thumbs up. "Can I go over that other one we have to send over right quick? I just thought of a twist."

"Damn I just see the time," Judah noted. "I have to go."

"Oh I got it," Mac told him.

Judah nodded then watched Shay as Mac set her up to sing again. In the past year, she had grown up so much. She'd even switched up her look with a nose piercing and straightened her curls. Now that his head was clear, he was able to correctly guide her as she secured her spot as a rising star and reminded her of the secular artists who still put a gospel single on their tracks.

"By the way, do you mind if I ask her out tonight?" Mac asked Judah as Shay continued.

"Yeah I do mind," Judah replied. "Where are you trying to take her?"

"For a drive, maybe walk down by the pier," he said. "Dinner by the food trucks she likes."

Judah had been quietly observing their chemistry and wondered when they were going to let it be known. He figured Mac was just making sure because he didn't want to mess up their professional relationship. Or maybe it was because he was a bit older than Shay he didn't want to come across as creepy.

"Sounds nice but I tell you what though, if you touch her or break her heart I'll break you," Judah warned him. "Screw her over, leave her with a kid, I'll break you harder. Don't like her today and then go back to them influencers or models tomorrow."

"Nah," he said. "She's not that type. She's special. Besides that wouldn't make no sense with her opportunities. I been in this game too long now. It's time I seriously settle. She's a little younger but she's special."

"You already know," Judah looked back at Shay. "Meanwhile it took you long enough to formally ask because I been watching you watch her for a couple of weeks. But you approached me as her father and I can respect that."

"I respect you bro," Mac said respectfully. "I respect her too."

"I got to go," Judah told him. "But yall can chill until you're ready." Judah grabbed his keys and rushed to the front door just as the doorbell rang. He was surprised to see Darold on the other side.

"Flight got in early so I got a rideshare," Darold walked in.

"Oh okay then," Judah hugged Darold. "Man it feels so good to hug you."

"Grandad grew a new leg!" Maya gasped walking by. "How'd you grow a new leg?"

"It's a miracle!" Darold said as she hugged him.

"Hi Ms Barbara," she hugged Barbara.

"Oh you remembered me!" Barbara hugged her back. "It looks like you have grown two inches since I've seen you."

"Yes ma'am," Maya smiled. "You want to see our pool?

"In a minute," Judah said, getting their luggage. "Y'all come in. Let me get y'all something to drink. Welcome to California, Barbara."

As Judah and Barbara chatted, Maya watched her grandfather with his walking cane head over to a chair and sit down.

"How come you can walk?" she asked. "Your leg was in the earthquake."

"It's a prosthetic," he said, pulling up his pant leg. "See. It's like a robot leg."

"Ohhh!" she leaned in to inspect it. "That makes sense."

"Where is your brother?" he asked.

"With Mommy," she replied.

"I'm right here," JJ said, greeting his grandfather.

Judah smiled as he watched their reunion and then told the children to give them a moment.

"Well now Mister bestselling author and platinum producer, it's good to see you," Darold pointed at his son. "I saw that interview. You let out a lot on your personal life and your brother. I wasn't all for it because I didn't want them judging you but you did good son. I am real proud of you."

"And the fan base saw me as authentic," Judah smiled. "I thought for sure they were done with me."

"Greater Gates is asking when you'll be coming through," Darold told him. "They are all missing you. They love you, son. By the way, you heard from your mother?"

"No sir," Judah said. "Have you?"

"Not since the divorce and she sent her attorney for that," Darold told him. "Don't know where she is and quite honestly I don't care. But moving on. Son, you know it's not good for a man to be alone. And when you've been living with a witch you tend to appreciate the angels a lot more. What I mean is… Well, just show him."

Barbara blushed but held out her hand to show an engagement ring.

"Ooh wee!" Judah beamed. "That's a big old rock you got there Barbara! I'm surprised the plane was able to take off. Well congratulations!"

"I know you said you're not performing any more but I'd be honored if you could sing at our wedding," Barbara said. "Thinking about it, I've never even seen you perform in person."

"Oh he got a whole recording studio down there," Darold said. "You ought to see him putting all that stuff together. Talented, that one is. Are you and Derika still okay? Where is she?"

"Yo Dee!" Judah shouted. "Come here! Daddy wants to show you something."

"Oh?" they heard Derika's footsteps. "Well, I got something to show him too."

"What's that you got there?" Darold asked, turning to where she was walking in.

"Come open those eyes and see your grandaddy, Joey," Judah said, taking their new baby from Derika's arms. "Support his head now, he's still little."

"All the babies I did christened I ain't never dropped," Darold teased holding his grandson. "Well look here! Took me over a month to see you in person, Joey. You got your uncle's name and your daddy's everything else. Looks just like you as an infant, Judah, even your hairline. Fine boy, you got here. Look at them wise eyes. That's the part he gets from me."

"How is Maya adjusting?" asked Barbara, peering at Joey.

"Better," Derika sighed. "She's still the only girl and Shay has been taking her to do girly things. She gets upset if Judah holds him too long or if he cries."

"She'll get over it," Barbara assured her. "Whenever you're ready, please let her come visit us."

"Are you sure?" Derika raised an eye. "She is a handful."

"We would love to have her," Barbara smiled.

"Now about this wedding," Judah asked. "Y'all two not in trouble and need to hurry up right?"

"At our age?" Barbara laughed. "It's interesting. I never had children of my own nor have I been married before. I was just always so busy with work."

"Daddy, JJ won't play with me," Maya walked in upset.

"Maya didn't you tell me about all those dolls last time I saw you?" Barbara asked.

"You remembered that?" she asked.

"Yes," Barbara smiled, going into her bag. "In fact, I thought this little one was lonely and could use a nice home."

Maya smiled when she saw the doll Barbara got for her.

"Thank you," Maya said. "I'm going to take her upstairs. We used to have a playroom but that's his room now. It's right next to my room. And he cries. All night long. They should've made his room soundproof too. It was nice when I only had a big brother not a loud baby."

"Maya!" Derika sighed.

"Well can you show me?" Barbara asked.

"Don't you want to stay and play with the baby?" Maya asked.

"After you show me the dolls," Barbara got up.

"Well go on Granny B," Judah laughed as she followed Maya.

"She finna stress y'all out," Darold laughed. "Ooh that's that southern sass!"

"Yeah…" Derika sighed. "That's the mean for no reason part of her I think she got from Lavinia. I can't wait for her to outgrow it."

"Nobody can put up with that level of mean forever," Darold sighed. "Forty-two years too long."

"Could we not?" Judah pleaded. "We agreed. Let go and let God."

"Darold, I want to hear more about this wedding," Derika smiled. "When did this whole thing blossom?"

"Yeah," Judah said as Joey started fussing. "You were clearly getting too much caregiving."

"Bring him here so I can feed him," Derika reached for Joey. "I'll be damned if your daughter tells me to keep him quiet so she can concentrate again."

Judah gently picked up the baby and rocked him a bit while singing quietly, calming him down. Joey stared at him for a moment, took a deep sigh, turned his head and opened his mouth.

"Nope," Judah laughed. "That's your mom not me."

He handed him to Derika who adjusted herself to nurse him.

"I told y'all how proud I am of y'all right?" Darold asked as he watched them. "Y'all continue on. You hear me?"

Judah sat next to Derika and put his arm around her as they listened to Darold. When they left Atlanta, they encountered heavy scrutiny and rumors, most blaming Derika for cheating and Judah for using her and the church to hide. Judah gave her an exit by filing for divorce. She contemplated it for about two months while Judah got back into producing and songwriting, finally focusing on his partnership with Pat. They both prayed for a sign to make things work and were surprised, but thrilled to learn their night of reconciliation resulted in conceiving a new life. At Pat's advice they did one magazine interview together making the cover. The television interview that followed was taped at the house but Derika stayed elusive and excused herself saying she needed to do something with the children.

Derika was much happier. She had completely cut off Cameron and was happy when he began showing up with a model on his arm. He never confirmed they had a relationship and worked with Ruby rather than her at Judah's request. There was a small part of Derika that felt more desired when she realized how jealous and angry Judah had gotten for keeping it from him and in a weird way, it actually strengthened them. She and Ruby created a management firm that Ruby ended up taking more control over as Derika opted to stay home with the children for a while. The Prescotts remained friends, visiting California now and again so the children could reconnect. As Joey's godmother, Fiona was also the trusted friend Derika needed whenever she wanted to just vent but receive advice from another woman. Paul expressed how proud he was of them and never judged their dynamic as long as they were both willing to work on their union.

Everyone had found exactly what they needed after the storms of the past two years finally seemed to settle.

Then there was Lavinia. No one really knew exactly what happened to Lavinia even though she kept up to date with what was going on from where she lived quietly with her brother in a small town. She was rather disappointed that life went on without her and no one reported her as missing. No one bothered them or knew of their past. She wanted to give her family and church a year to really need her. After seeing how happy they were with a new baby and a new bride in the family, posing at Greater Gates together as a happy family, she had enough and decided life without the spotlight and without her family wasn't worth it anymore. Rather than give them the satisfaction of seeing her defeated, she slipped away silently, swearing to never think of them again.

As they relaxed in bed together with their older children between them later that night, the baby sleeping on Judah's chest, Derika smiled. She thought of all the sacrifices they agreed to for the simple moments like this one. She wondered what the next twenty years would bring. She didn't know that Darold would still be there proud of everything they did. While she knew Shay would still be in their lives, she didn't see just how things would change but eventually be okay with them. She didn't know that while he'd never sing a note, that JJ would end up creating his own label and running both of his parents' companies. Her newborn Joey would become the standout star, breaking Judah's musical records. She didn't realize that she would eventually end up back in church with Maya as a pastor and gospel singer, inspired by her childhood memories of her aunt and uncle to do things with pure intentions. The one thing she did know was that she and Judah would be older but still together cheering on each other.

"You good?" Judah asked Derika as Joey stretched.

"Want me to put him in the crib?" she asked.

"Nah," Judah said looking at the older children nibbling on popcorn. "We all good. Just here. In it together."

"Always," she said as they shared a kiss.

ABOUT THE AUTHOR

Arthia Nixon is an award-winning journalist turned Atlanta-based publicist/consultant whose first love remains writing.

In addition to her children's books such as "Da Magic Grouper and Dem" being on some school curricula in the Caribbean, she also coaches and represents other authors with their media placement.

Her novella 'Elevators', initially intended to be a stand-alone paved the way for 'Drawn Curtains', 'Snagged Threads' and 'The Grieving Billionaire' introduced readers to her signature style for suspenseful steamy dramatic romantic juicy page-turners with a dash of wit,

In her spare time, she enjoys tea, traveling, beaching and being the author of her own adventures. She spends her time between homes in Georgia and her native Bahamas and on set as a momager. More on www.arthianixon.com